Cowboy's Break

Cowboy's Break

LEXI POST

Poker Flat Book 4

Copyright © 2016 by Lexi Post

This book is a work of fiction. The names, characters, places, and incidents are products of the writer's imagination or have been used fictitiously and are not to be construed as real. Any resemblance to persons, living or dead, actual events, locales or organizations is entirely coincidental.

ALL RIGHTS RESERVED. No part of this book may be used or reproduced in any manner whatsoever without written permission from the author.

For information contact Lexi Post at www.lexipostbooks.com

Cover design by Bella Media Management

Cover photo: Cover Me, Becky McGraw

Cover model: Stephen Pierce

ISBN: 978-1-949007-12-1

Excerpt of *Wedding at Poker Flat* © 2018 by Lexi Post

Cowboy's Break

(Poker Flat, Book #4)

By Lexi Post

Cowboy and former detective Vince Gallagher never thought he'd have a second chance to convince Rachel Henderson they were meant to be together, nor did he think he'd want to. Now, after seven years, thanks to his old police academy friend, Vince is knee deep in numbers and computers, determined to save Rachel's ranch and his own heart.

Rachel hadn't expected to see Vince again…ever. In fact, she planned on it. Saying goodbye to him had been the hardest thing she'd ever done, but she couldn't handle her sister, the ranch, and his job as an undercover detective all at the same time. Now she's with him every day and buried feelings just won't go away.

The closer Vince gets to solving the mystery of the missing money, the more convinced he becomes that Rachel is the one for him. But when prize animals start disappearing, he has to choose between revealing the culprit and keeping the woman he's always loved from harm. He just can't catch a break.

Acknowledgments

For my own cowboy, Bob Fabich, the best cook in our house.

For Paige Wood, who reads anything I write, even the not so perfect.

A huge thank you to Marie Patrick, a wonderful friend and a fantastic critique partner.

Author's Note

Cowboy's Break is part of the Poker Flat series which was inspired by Bret Harte's short story, *The Outcasts of Poker Flat*, first published in 1869. In Harte's story, four members of Poker Flat society—a gambler, a prostitute, a madam, and a drunk--are banned from the western settlement when a sudden urge to be virtuous overtakes the citizens. On their way to the next settlement, the outcasts stop to rest at the base of some high mountains. An innocent couple, a young man and his fiancée (a tavern waitress), comes down from the mountains and rests with them. This cast of characters explores the relationship between the innocent and the tainted in Harte's story.

What if things just don't work out for the innocents? And what if the plans of one who is tainted threatens their second chance at forever?

Chapter One

Rachel Henderson sucked in her breath as the door to the diner opened and a tall cowboy strode in. What the hell was Vince Gallagher doing here?

His chiseled jaw and boyish good looks hid a mature man of strong character and confidence. She knew better than anyone exactly how experienced and loyal he was.

"Rachel? What are you looking at?" Hunter McKade waved his hand in front of her eyes. He was a family friend that went back as far as her first tricycle and he effectively pulled her attention away from the man scanning the crowd.

She turned her head in the futile hope Vince wouldn't see her. "Nothing. Just people coming and going."

Her answer wasn't nearly clever enough for Hunter. The man had been in Afghanistan and a police officer before that. He could tell right away she lied.

Hunter looked over his shoulder and around the wall behind him. "Vince! Over here."

As he waved, Rachel's stomach turned over and her mouth went dry. She couldn't do this. "*He's* the friend you said could help me?" Her voice rose to a much higher pitch than normal.

Hunter turned back toward her. "Yes. Vince Gallagher is the best there is when it comes to detective work that involves finances." He paused. "Are you okay? You've lost your tan in three seconds." He paused again, studying her. "Do you know Vince?"

She grabbed her purse. "I think it's the creamer. I'm going to the restroom." She slid out of the booth they occupied and stood. Vince was barely ten feet away and he stopped as recognition dawned.

"Rachel?" His baritone voice sent memories kaliedoscoping through her mind.

She spun around and strode to the ladies room, her heart beating a two-step in her chest as she expected his hand to clamp down on her shoulder at any moment and stop her. Pulling open the bathroom door, she glanced back as it closed.

Vince stood rock still where she'd left him.

She locked the door and walked to the sink, her breathing ragged from her surprise. Running the water, she scooped it up and rinsed her face. As the water dripped off, she looked in the mirror.

"You need to get a hold of yourself, woman." She snorted. "As if that's gonna happen."

Vince Gallagher was the only man she'd ever

loved…still loved. And it hadn't been that superficial love based on his warm brown eyes, dark brown hair and toned physique. She'd broken both their hearts over seven years ago when he'd worked for the Austin police force.

He'd gone into a deep and dangerous undercover operation and after almost three months of worrying and wondering if he was alive, she'd known she couldn't live like that. She'd embarrassed both of them by repeatedly going to his chief and asking if he'd heard anything.

"You were a weak, pathetic girl, Rachel Henderson." She grabbed a couple paper towels and wiped her face and hands. While Vince was undercover, her father had died of a heart attack, her mother was diagnosed with stage-four cancer and her sister had become pregnant at the ripe age of seventeen.

When Vince finally emerged from the operation, it had been a full six months. He'd come to her expecting a happy reunion, but she couldn't do it. He'd wanted to help, but his job came first. He was good at his job and she hadn't wanted him to have to choose. "Yup, you made the decision for him, didn't you? That's what every man wants, a woman who decides for him. He's got to hate you by now."

Her heart lurched. She thought she'd buried those feelings six feet under, but obviously there wasn't enough dirt in all of Daisy Creek to keep them repressed.

She still loved him. He'd accepted her for who she was, a rancher's daughter, no more, no less.

"You're an idiot." She scowled at herself in the

mirror. "The most noble, good-hearted cowboy in all of central Texas and you kicked him out of your life. Good job." And now, that man was here because her childhood friend had called him to help her. Her!

"Nice, this should go well. Hi, Vince. Sorry about breaking your heart. Now could you help me save my ranch?"

She looked at her purse sitting on the sink counter, the insufficient funds notice folded up inside. She'd called Hunter's mom to find out where he was and had been surprised to discover his wife had died and he was living with a woman and working at Poker Flat, a nudist resort in Arizona. She hadn't seen that coming. But if anyone could help her, she'd known he could.

Hunter arrived and looked over what she had. When he said he had a friend nearby from his police academy days who had specialized in financial investigations, she breathed a lot easier. She couldn't lose her ranch. It and her sister were all she had left of her family.

Now she could barely get air past her lungs. She didn't want to face Vince again. Already the feelings she had for him were floating toward the top, cresting over the walls she'd built around her heart.

She had a decision to make. Face him and save her ranch or ditch his help and try to manage on her own. The problem was, if Hunter couldn't figure it out after looking over everything for the last three days then how could she?

She *had* to save the ranch. That was her mantra since she called Hunter. It was the only stability she had and she worked hard through everything to hold on to it. Her sister, though not at the ranch every day, called it home. Crystal had helped to keep it from bankruptcy once before because she loved it.

"You told Hunter you'd do anything to keep it." She frowned at herself. "So are you still the weak pathetic girl from seven years ago?" She nodded at herself. "No, you're not. Now go out there and face your issues head on."

Right. She stared hard at herself before noticing she'd plastered tiny strands of her blonde hair across her forehead and she had a piece of hay stuck on her sleeve. Impatiently, she pushed her hair back into place and threw the hay in the trash.

Other than that, she looked pretty much the same as the last time she saw Vince.

She shrugged. "What's it matter. You're not going on a date. He already knows you have no waist, too-long legs and an ass that's bigger than it should be. Stop stalling."

Giving herself a final scowl in the mirror, she picked up her purse and moved to the door. *You can do this*. She could accept Vince's help if he was willing to give it. He would be working with Hunter, after all, and not her.

She opened the door and halted. What if he hated her? She gripped the handle as her stomach roiled. *Please don't hate me.*

Maybe he would refuse to help. Or maybe Vince had much better things to do than help an old girlfriend who had dumped him. A man's ego could only take so much.

She swallowed the lump in her throat. She could play

"what if" all day, but all she had to do is walk a hundred feet and get her questions answered. Slowly, she released the door and moved toward the table.

Vince walked into the diner and his heart lurched at the sight of Rachel Henderson. For a split second he gazed into Rachel's blue eyes, her face unchanged over the years except for a darker tan, her skin still satiny, and her chin still stubborn.

Then she walked away from him…again. Her hips swaying and her pale blonde braid swishing right and left with her gait.

His gut twisted. Was she married now? Did she have a husband and children who helped her with Sunnyview Ranch? Was the man of her heart easier to "handle" than he was? Anger rushed over him and he gritted his teeth.

Finally, he turned to look at Hunter, who stood studying him. Damn, he hoped the investigation wasn't about Rachel's husband cheating on her. His hands fisted of their own accord.

"So are you going to give an old friend a welcome or just stand there like a statute all day?" Hunter's lips quirked up at the corner.

Vince relaxed his hands and gave his friend a one-armed hug. When they parted, he shook his head. "Wow, you are just full of surprises."

"I hadn't planned on that. So you know Rachel?" Hunter motioned to the empty seat across from him and sat.

"Yes." Vince slid into the booth.

Hunter raised his brow. "That's it?"

"Tell you what, you tell me why you're dressed like Johnny Cash and I'll tell you about Rachel."

Hunter grimaced. "It could just be that I like black."

"I don't think so." He waved at a waitress who gave him the "be right there sign." "So why the black? Did you lose someone overseas?" Though he and Hunter had taken different paths after the police department, they heard about each other on occasion.

His old friend remained silent a moment before taking a breath. "Julie was killed."

"What?" Shit, Julie and Hunter had been made for each other. He'd been a groomsman at their wedding. Hunter had found himself the perfect woman. "What happened?"

"Drunk driver."

"Fuck." He could feel Hunter's anger even from across the table, and he didn't blame him. He was furious himself.

Hunter took a deep breath, and with it his body relaxed. "I've been lucky though. Found another woman just right for me. The complete opposite of Julie, but she's what I need now."

Vince studied Hunter. The man really had found someone else. "What do you mean, what you need now?" The waitress came over and he ordered a coffee. When she left, he tilted his head. "So?"

"It's hard to explain. War changes a person. Adriana is a good fit for me now, but if I'd met her when I was on the force, well, I wouldn't have been interested."

"Ah, now that I do understand." His days of

undercover work had changed him as well and probably not for the better.

A man could only see so much violence, killing… blood before it affected him. The scream of a woman resounded in his ears as his mind recalled her fall from a nineteenth story balcony. Her dealer had pushed her. He could still hear the sound of her body hitting a car below. He tried to tell himself that he'd made a difference, but he didn't believe it.

He hated the unwanted memories and shook his head to clear it. "So you wear black in Julie's memory?"

Hunter smirked. "No, I just got used to it."

Vince chuckled before looking over his shoulder toward the restrooms where Rachel had disappeared.

Hunter pushed his half-eaten churro away and picked up his coffee. "How do you know Rachel?"

Know her? I loved her. He shrugged. "We dated for a while, but undercover work isn't conducive to a relationship."

It was obvious Hunter wasn't buying his offhand story, but he didn't push the issue. "Still doing that?"

"No. Quit that a few years ago to set up shop with a friend." He still felt like his current partner, Roscoe Donati, had saved his ass by offering him the chance to start an investigation agency. "Who knew there would be so much need for investigative skills in the ranch land of Texas? Our main client is the Oteros, but we take on a few other clients here and there. Believe me, the Oteros keep us hopping."

"The Oteros? I remember them. They have a big

spread near Bandera, right? I went to school with Esteban. Seemed like a decent guy. I was in a couple rodeos with Joseph. He lived life on the edge. Is he still alive?"

Vince nodded. "Yes, he is. He's settled down some. A good woman will do that to you."

Hunter's mouth quirked up again as if in silent amusement.

He gestured with his thumb over his shoulder. "Is Rachel the person you mentioned on the phone who needed my help?"

Hunter looked past him and frowned. "Yes. She's a very old friend." He returned his attention to the conversation. "I've known her my whole life and she's in trouble. I flew in to see what I could do, but I could use your help."

"If Rachel needs help, I'm in." No matter his feelings toward her now, he couldn't just walk away.

Hunter raised a brow but didn't comment on his willingness.

She could have called *him*. He certainly called her plenty of times, but she never answered after she broke it off. She even changed her phone number.

"Good." Hunter looked up. "Then I'll let her explain the situation."

He smelled the scent of leather and lavender before he turned around.

She avoided his gaze and slipped into the booth next to Hunter. She was more beautiful than he remembered, high cheekbones, a strong straight nose and pale pink lips, which at the moment, were pursed together.

Her shoulders were back, her posture always straight,

and the short sleeved tan top she wore paled against her skin. She was still riding and getting her hands dirty. Not one of those ranch owners who let "the boys" do all the work. That didn't surprise him. As he gazed at her, every feeling he'd ever had rose up to choke him.

Come on. Look at me.

The silence became awkward, Hunter clearly not willing to get involved in what was between them.

He took the bull by the horns. "It's good to see you, Rachel." Her gaze snapped to his when he spoke her name. "I told Hunter I'd be willing to help in any way I can. Tell me what's going on."

She appeared on the verge of tears, and it took everything he had to keep himself on the other side of the table. He wanted to hold her and tell her everything would be all right. She was a strong woman, so if she was this low, it had to be big.

"It's the Sunnyview." She looked down at her hands which were clasped on the table. "I'm going to lose it if I can't discover where all the money's gone."

Hell, that ranch meant everything to her and he knew it. It had been the main reason she'd dumped him. She'd said it was all she could handle. "What happened?"

She reached into her purse, pulled out a bank notice and handed it to him. His breath went out between his teeth. There were five insufficient funds notices on very large payments and one was to the state for quarterly taxes.

This was no laughing matter. "I have to ask, were you aware that you didn't have enough funds or miscalculated the date income was coming in?" With his partner, he was the one who usually asked the questions no one wanted to voice.

"If I'd known I didn't have enough funds, I wouldn't be here." She glared at him. "I know how to manage a ranch and a business. I've reviewed my books and they are accurate to the cent. There should have been over forty thousand dollars in that particular account."

She pulled the paper from his hand and refolded it. "I immediately went to our other accounts and there are similar discrepancies. I think I'm being hacked and it must have started this month because all the past bank statements balance out."

Hunter leaned forward. "The only people besides Rachel who can access those accounts are her sister, her accountant, and her foreman."

He looked at her, the investigative side of his brain fully engaged now. "You say you think it's a hacker. Why? Why not your sister, the accountant or your foreman?"

"First of all, my sister depends on the money the ranch makes to supplement her income, so she certainly isn't going to sabotage that." Rachel's brows drew together. "Besides, she *is* my sister. Second, my accountant has been with me for over ten years now and is the accountant for a couple other much bigger ranches. We've had no problems up to this point with her. Lastly, Sam has been with me for more than seven years and has been my right-hand man. If Sunnyview goes under, he's out of a job and he has a family."

Vince leaned back, his mind racing with possibilities for all three of the people she ruled out. Emergencies, change in living circumstances, even blackmail could cause a person to act out of character and do something he or she usually wouldn't do.

But he wouldn't have that conversation now or Rachel would warn those people he would be looking into their behind-the-scenes lives. He was surprised, however, by her conclusion. "If we rule out those people, then why do you think it's a hacker? Why not a bank employee? Or a stranger who looked over your shoulder?"

Rachel's shoulders fell. "It's just a guess. I don't know who else it could be and since the Oteros were hacked recently and I sell to them, I figure maybe that gave the hacker access to my accounts." She raised a shoulder, clearly at a loss and his heart engaged again.

He reached across the table and placed his hand over her clasped ones. He didn't fail to notice the roughened edges of her knuckles. "Don't worry. We'll get this figured out."

She pulled her hands into her lap and looked at Hunter. "That's why I called you. I might be able to figure this out, but by the time I did, I'd be broke." She turned to Vince. "I moved funds from the other accounts to make new payments, but there's not much left. I have no money to hire anyone. I don't want to take a loan out against the ranch. The news would spread like wildfire in this town. In Daisy Creek, everyone knows everyone else."

He gave her a steady look, the idea that he would charge was a kick to his gut, but she didn't need to know that. He moved his gaze to Hunter. "I'd like to take the lead on this case."

"Sounds good."

"No."

The contradictory responses were no surprise. Hunter elbowed Rachel lightly. "Rache, listen. You know I'd do anything for you, but I know what I don't know. My computer and finance knowledge is no better than yours. I couldn't find anything this weekend either, but I'll still stay at the ranch and help with the investigation. Adriana is busy training a new bartender and if she misses me too much, she'll just show up on your doorstep."

Hunter's lips quirked up slightly as if he hoped his girlfriend would do exactly that. The two of them really did need to catch up.

He piggybacked on Hunter's statement. "I'll tackle the behind the scene issues as that is my expertise."

Hunter broke in. "You know what we called him on the police force?"

Rachel shook her head, but still didn't look at him.

"*The arranger.* If you needed something done with no one knowing about it, Vince was your man. I'm sure you want to keep this issue quiet. Texas is a big state of small towns."

She rolled her eyes. "That's one way of putting it. You're lucky you moved."

"Where are you now?" Vince had two reasons for asking. One he was curious, but more importantly, he wanted to gauge which people he could have Hunter tail. The man was quieter than the wind.

"I'm in Arizona now. Working security for Pocker Flat Nudist Resort."

Vince was well versed in hiding his feelings, but he couldn't help widening his eyes at that. "A nudist resort?"

Hunter shrugged. "I don't have to worry about people hiding guns in their clothing there."

Understanding dawned. His friend had served two tours in Afghanistan. That had to have an impact on a man. He wanted to ask how he was doing, but didn't. Since he had his own demons to contend with, maybe a couple beers with an old friend might put some of them to sleep, but not in front of Rachel. They'd only reconnected because of her.

He focused on Rachel and caught her studying him, but she looked away. She wouldn't be able to hide for long. "I've got a couple loose ends to tie up for the Oteros this morning, but I'll drive out this afternoon and start looking at your books. I'll need user names and passwords to all your accounts."

"The Oteros?" Her whole body stiffened. "I didn't know you worked for them."

He nodded. "Good. You aren't supposed to. Roscoe and I work for them privately."

She squinted at him. "Did you know I sell cattle to the Oteros?"

"Yes. I know everything there is to know about their operation and a lot about their family."

She sat back in surprise, but he couldn't tell if it

was because he'd left her alone like she wished, or if she couldn't believe he'd really known about her connection to the family. He'd known for years, but she'd made it clear when she changed her phone number that they were more than done.

Now fate had brought them together and he would move mountains if he had to in order to save her ranch. But they would have a talk. He wanted closure on their relationship. This time he wasn't going anywhere until he decided it was time to go.

Chapter Two

Rachel didn't understand the ache in her chest since she'd left Vince and Hunter at the diner and headed home. He'd known they worked with the same family and had stayed away. She should feel grateful, but part of her was crushed.

"Shit, Rachel, he did what you told him to do. He stayed away. You have no reason to be hurt that he kept his word. He's a damn cowboy for criminy sake. What'd you expect?"

Her double cab pick-up hit a rut and bounced her up, almost hitting her head on the ceiling. That rut had been there since last month's wash out.

"Good job. Now you can't even drive with him on your mind." That was part of the problem seven years ago. He filled her every waking thought and even half her nighttime ones. She'd been a mess wondering if he was alive or dead while she tried to keep her little sister out of trouble after her dad died. She'd failed at that, too.

Her mother probably could have fought the cancer, but she had no will to live. The second her dad was gone, her mom handed everything over to her. To this day, she was thankful she'd already graduated college. Her sister was in her senior year of high school and the death of their father hadn't helped her emotional state.

Driving the truck up to the porch that ran the length of the two-story ranch house, Rachel parked it. She stared at her home. It wasn't huge, just four bedrooms upstairs with the living room, long kitchen and den downstairs, but it had seen so much love. The outside was still in good shape as well. The pale blue painted clapboard siding contrasted nicely with the white shutters and trim, but what made it home was the memories.

Two rockers sat on one end of the porch where her parents used to spend time quietly talking after dinner while she and Crystal rocked in the big porch swing on the other end. Even she and Vince had spent some time in that swing. Her body heated and she quickly turned the truck off and opened the door.

Would coming back here bring painful memories for him, too? He loved her parents as if they were his own. They practically were since he had no real parents. That he'd turned out so well despite that fact had always attracted her to him. "Stop mooning over something that was never meant to be. You have work to do."

She jumped out and grabbed a bag of groceries and her purse.

"Need some help, Miss Rachel?" Sam strode out

of the horse barn, his bowlegged walk giving him an awkward gait. The smile beneath his heavy mustache never let on that he'd just started physical therapy to get more mobility. Like every stubborn cowboy, he'd refused to go to the doc's when he was younger and now at forty-two, he was paying for it.

"Thanks. There's two more bags on the other side."

As Sam moved to the passenger door, she brought the bag of cold food through the farmhouse and into the kitchen. Plunking it down on the twelve foot oak table that was the long kitchen's centerpiece, she opened the refrigerator.

Why hadn't she asked Hunter who he was calling in to help her? He'd been living in Arizona for so many years, she never expected he'd bring in Vince.

She set the milk on the second shelf. The man was just as broad and confident as he was when they'd been close. Hell, who was she kidding? They'd been lovers with a whole future ahead of them. She'd always told herself it was just bad timing—his undercover work, her dad's and mom's deaths, the ranch responsibilities, her sister's drama.

He'd wanted to help, but he was gone for six months. That wasn't a man she could depend on. She'd been right to break it off. It wouldn't have—

"Ah, Miss Rachel, aren't you too young to be having them hot flash things?" Sam put the other two bags of groceries down on the table.

"What?"

He pointed to the open refrigerator door. "I know

the fridge here is cool, but you could turn up the air conditioner."

She closed the door and shook her head. "No, I was just thinking."

Sam's gaze grew shrewd. "Men or money?"

Whoa, he was way too close. It was both and neither if her account was any gauge. "Just thinking about the Oteros' cattle order. Did Aron call yet?"

Sam smiled at her, clearly not buying her story, but he was too much of a gentlemen to push it. "No, but I was riding the north fence and the reception is spotty." He pulled his cellphone from his belt and looked at it. "Nope, no calls." He smiled. "But I did get a text from Eva."

"Your six year-old daughter is texting?" She returned to the grocery bag with cold food in it and continued emptying it.

He flipped the phone around so she could see. "Actually, she posed for Marie and made her send the picture."

Rachel looked at the photo of the little girl in a ballet outfit posing while leaning on one crutch. She'd fallen out of a tree two weeks ago and broke her leg. She was a handful. "She's growing up so fast."

He looked at the phone once again then clipped it back to his belt. "Yeah. I'm just glad I get to go home every night. Some of the men here are working two jobs."

Her stomach tightened. She paid her cowboys well, but it wasn't anything a person could buy a house with or start a family with. She'd actually hoped to give raises come calving season, but that didn't look good now. "How are the feed levels?"

"They're fine. I've got the herefords out in the west pasture. There's good eating out there right now."

Thank the Lord for that. She should probably tell Sam that Vince was coming over, so he wouldn't wonder like he had when Hunter showed up. She'd expected her old friend to advise her over the phone and the next morning he was on her doorstep. Since Hunter's sister was older than him, he liked playing big brother to her and right now she was fine with that.

She pulled another grocery bag toward her. "We're going to be having more company today. Do you remember Vince Gallagher?"

Sam's widening eyes said more than he did. "Yeah."

She turned to put the bags of beans away and spoke over her shoulder. "It turns out he's an old friend of Hunter's. He's going to stop by." She had to turn back and face Sam to get another item out of the bag.

He stared at her, a frown on his face. "Yeah?"

She nodded and quickly grabbed the spaghetti from the bag. "Yes. The two of them are working on, uh… something." She couldn't tell him the ranch was in trouble thanks to the missing money. She didn't want to worry him unless absolutely necessary.

"Miss Rachel, we all know you had a thing for Vince. Are you sure you're okay with this?"

She nodded but wouldn't look him in the eye. Any reference to Vince sent her heartbeat racing. She hadn't told anyone yet of the bounced checks. She'd rather keep it between herself and her creditors. She burrowed into the bottom of the grocery bag and pulled out the chocolate chips she'd bought. "I think I'll make my monster cookies for the men today. Hunter always did like Mom's homemade treats." *But Vince is the one who loved her monster cookies the most.*

"I'm sure they'll appreciate that." Sam remained silent while she started unpacking the other bag. Finally, he shook his head. "Well, I better get back to work. If you need me, just holler."

"Thanks, I will." She didn't look up, not willing to let him know how rattled she was. She was the owner of the Sunnyview Ranch. It was her responsibility to take care of things and if that meant having Vince in her house again, then she'd just have to suck it up and deal with it.

She'd just put away the last of the groceries when she caught sight of a dust cloud coming up the dirt driveway. She grinned. Just what the doctor ordered, a bit of sunshine from her little sister.

Crystal had a rough time in high school, and losing her baby had sent her into a worse depression than when their dad died. Then there were the drugs she'd used to cope. But after seeing a psychiatrist, she'd finally come into her own in college, graduating with a degree in accounting. She was a whiz with numbers and had finessed a few deals over the years to benefit the ranch.

When the convertible came to a stop, Rachel walked out onto the porch. Her sister came by two or three times a week, always unannounced and always welcome.

"Hey, Rache!" Crystal waved from the driver seat

before stepping out onto the hard-packed dirt that served as the front yard in a pair of red strappy heels, a knee length floral dress and a dozen bangles on her wrists. Her hair was golden blonde and despite the wind from the drive, fell perfectly about her shoulders. "We really need to pave that driveway."

Rachel laughed. "That would look pretty funny having a paved driveway off a dirt road that comes to a dirt yard."

Her sister sauntered up the steps and gave her a hug, the knock-off perfume she wore engulfing them both in hyacinth. It smelled wonderful.

"Good point. Guess I'll just have to learn to put the top up." Crystal shrugged her shoulders and moved toward the door. "Is Hunter still here?"

She followed her sister into the house all the way to the kitchen in back. "Yes, I think he's staying a few more days. He's catching up with old friends."

Crystal went to the refrigerator and took out the sweet tea. "Did he say why he wasn't staying with his parents?" She poured the tea into a tall glass and put the pitcher away.

Rachel sat at the table, in no hurry to tell her sister what she'd received from the bank. Not yet anyway. She didn't want to worry her either, plus Crystal wouldn't take it well. She hated making mistakes and if this was her mistake, Rachel wasn't sure how she'd handle it. "Hunter said he wasn't ready to see them. He's still working through his wife's death and everything he went through overseas."

Crystal raised an eyebrow. "Are you sure he's taken again?"

"Absolutely. Besides, he's far too old for you."

"Of course, he is. I didn't mean for me." She winked and took a sip of tea.

"Oh, no." Rachel waved her hand as she shook her head. "We're just friends, like brother and sister. Don't even go there."

Her sister pouted then brightened. "Hey, then why don't you come down to Big Joe's Friday night. They're having a live band and there'll be two-stepping and lots of cowboys."

It sounded great, but her party days were over as quickly as they'd started. "I'll see."

Crystal pulled out a chair across from her and sat, crossing her legs and staring at her. "That means you plan to put on one of your oversized t-shirts and curl up on the couch with a book or a movie. Come on, sis. You need to interact with more than just Sam and the guys. You're becoming a recluse."

"Hah." She snorted, not caring how unladylike she sounded. "I'll have you know I went to the diner this morning and the grocery store afterwards. See, I do get out."

"Very funny." Crystal gave her a saucy look before taking another sip of her tea. "I came by because I can't work on the books until this weekend, so I thought I'd check and see if you needed any bills paid before then."

Shit. She rose and walked to the fridge as she answered. "No, I'm good." She pulled out the sweet tea.

"I didn't realize how dry I was until I saw you drinking this." She pulled a glass from the cupboard and poured herself the tawny liquid. She actually *was* thirsty. "How's work going?"

When Crystal didn't answer, she looked over her shoulder at her. She was staring out the window.

Following her sister's gaze, Rachel swallowed hard. Vince had driven up and stood chatting with one of her men who'd just ridden in. She glanced at the clock. It couldn't be after noon yet, could it?

She was wrong. It was five past the hour. She'd forgotten how punctual he was.

"Rache, do you have something you want to tell me?" Crystal stared at her, her brow knit with worry, her light brown eyes concerned.

She waved her off and leaned her hips against the counter, crossing one arm over her waist as she took a sip of tea. "It's nothing. Vince is working with Hunter on a project."

Her sister's gaze didn't move. "And you're okay with this? I thought you never wanted to see him again?"

She hadn't, but she'd never told Crystal why. She didn't want her feeling guilty. "It's been a long time. I'm fine." *And I'm a big fat liar.*

She put her glass on the counter and headed around the table.

Crystal's hand shot out and grabbed her wrist. "Hey, there's no rush." She looked back at the window. "He's busy. Tell me why you never wanted to see him again. I was so wrapped up in my own problems back then, I didn't pay attention to yours."

She glanced out the window, stalling for time. What could she say? "It was his job. He went deep undercover for six months and I had no way of knowing if he was dead or alive. I couldn't be in a relationship with someone who did that on a regular basis. It was too heartbreaking."

Crystal let her wrist go. "That makes a lot of sense. Do you still have feelings for him?"

She shrugged. "It doesn't matter. That was a long time ago. We both have our separate lives now."

"You didn't answer my question, which means yes." Crystal's shrewd gaze softened. "You want me to show him in?"

Yes. "No, I can handle it. He's probably already married to some sweet thing who goes to her parents' house whenever he goes undercover." She strode out of the room.

If he goes undercover. She almost tripped on the braided rug in the living room at her thought. He said he did work for the Oteros. Did that mean he didn't put himself in danger anymore? The thought had her heart racing. "Rachel Henderson just stop thinking about what could have been. It's water under the bridge."

She shook her head and fisted her hands. He probably had a wife. She needed to focus on the ranch and keep her heart out of it.

She took a deep breath and continued through the living room, past the white leather furniture her mother said was a compromise between her father's request for leather and her mom's need for dainty, and on through to the front door. It was one of those beautiful spring afternoons in Texas that were so rare and so welcome. Sam had left the main door open and a light breeze came through the screen.

Vince still spoke to her ranch hand, his stance relaxed as he leaned against the corral fence. When he smiled at something her worker said, she smiled too. He had such a young looking face, always had, but it had clean lines, his jaw strong with a slight cleft in his chin, his nose straight, his lips perfect and his brown hair cut very short. He was the epitome of the Texas cowboy in looks and heart. She sighed.

"What are you doing mooning over a man you dumped?" Shaking her head, she took another deep breath and pushed the screen door open. He was here to find her missing money and then he'd go back to wherever he'd been and whoever he was with.

The door slammed behind her and Vince's gaze snapped to her. He nodded to her ranch hand then headed for her. His stride was purposeful, even more confident than it was years ago. His hair was shorter, but his face hadn't aged at all.

What must he think of her? Absently, she tucked a strand of hair behind her ear.

Just watching him walk flooded her with memories. The first time he came to take her out, he'd given her father complete deference and charmed her mother until she blushed.

The Sundays he joined them for dinners, his quick smile even made her sulky sister participate. He'd loved them all, not just her. Her mom jokingly said he'd adopted them.

The day he'd offered to fill in for a sick ranch hand and came in from the north pasture, took his shirt off, and soaked it with the hose to wring it out over his chest was the first night they made love, under the stars. She couldn't resist him.

"It's good to see you again." His low, soothing voice pulled her from her memories and caused her cheeks to heat.

"I didn't know Hunter called you. He just said he had someone who could help."

A flash of disappointment entered his eyes and was gone. "And I can. Why don't you show me everything?"

Shit, she'd been a little rude. She opened the door, and he took it in one hand as he doffed his hat with the other. She headed for her office across from the living room, his long strides on the wood floors behind her resonating with his masculinity throughout the house.

They entered the hall to find Crystal standing in the door to the office. "Hey Vince, it's been a long time." She looked him up and down as if judging if he was man enough to be there.

Really? Rachel stepped back so Vince could see her sister.

He nodded politely. "Crystal, you've grown up. How are you?"

She flashed him a quick smile. "I'm great." Then her eyebrows lowered. "But if you break my sister's heart again, I'll make you pay."

"Crystal!" Rachel felt a flush rise from her chest to her face. "He's working on a project with Hunter. He's not here for me."

The two of them ignored her and stared at each other.

Vince shook his head. "I never broke her heart, Crys. She broke mine. I'm just here because Hunter asked me."

"Fair enough." Crystal stepped away from the door toward Rachel. "See you this weekend, but if you need anything…" She paused as she looked at Vince, "just let me know."

"I will." Rachel embraced her sister then watched her walk into the living room, the flounce of her floral dress the last to disappear around the corner. Finally, she had to look at Vince and when she did, she wished she hadn't. His warm brown eyes revealed pain, which had a lump forming in her throat.

What could she say? She swallowed hard. "I'm sorry about that. She's grown up in some ways and not in others."

"Like I told her, I'm here to help in whatever way I can." His face revealed nothing.

She couldn't keep looking at him without her body tingling and her heart racing. So she stepped into her office and pulled out the big leather chair that used to be her father's.

She hadn't changed the room much. The memory of her father helped her keep going when things turned difficult and right now they were very difficult. "Here's the computer Crystal and I use for running the ranch.

We both have our own laptops, of course, for more personal business."

She walked over to a cabinet and opened the doors. "Bank statements are in this drawer, orders are in this binder, bills are over here, and past years' financials are over here in this cabinet. I think that's all you'll need."

She reached over and turned on the desktop computer. "All the passwords will automatically populate if you enter my name, Rae." She flushed. He was the only one who ever called her Rae. Quickly, she turned around to point out where the backup drive was when he caught her by the shoulders.

"Rae, look at me."

Reluctantly, she raised her gaze to meet his. The concern she found there unnerved her.

"You don't have to be afraid of me. I'm here to help."

"I'm not afraid of you. It's just awkward." She pulled away from him and leaned back against her dad's bookcase, a good five feet away from him.

"You mean because you dumped me." Vince's face hardened.

"I didn't dump you. I ended our relationship. And I'm glad I did. I was a mess and things got worse. After mom died, Crystal went into a tailspin and we had that drought putting us in the red. It was all I could do to hold this place together."

He stepped toward her but stopped when she put her hand out. "I could have helped you."

She shook her head. "No, you couldn't. You had to work. And you were good at what you did. Being around then disappearing for months wouldn't have helped. I had to do it on my own."

He opened his mouth then snapped it shut. The silence was deafening.

Finally, she pulled away from the bookcase. "Hunter tells me you're still good." She opened her arm toward the computer. "This is everything I have to do with the financials of the operation. I'll let you do what you do best. Solve problems." She strode past him to the door, thankful he didn't try to stop her. "I have to make cookies now."

Chapter Three

Vince remained where he was, still reeling from Rachel's words. She'd killed their relationship because of his job? She'd never told him that. She said she was too busy to focus on them, and when he offered to help, she shrugged him off.

He'd put it up to her independent nature. He called once in a while to see if she was finally ready, letting her know he was there if she needed him, but she never returned his calls. When she changed her number, he finally backed off.

She dumped him because of his job? He looked around the room, as if the books and computer and knick-knacks could answer his question. It was hard being the wife of an officer. He'd known that. Hell, Rachel and he had talked about the danger he was in. She was always concerned, but appeared confident in his abilities.

He moved to the large leather chair and sat down at

the computer. He didn't turn it on. She was right, he was good at it. That's why they'd sent him in deep undercover to rat out a huge drug-money laundering operation. He was supposed to just be the boss's numbers man, but he'd witnessed too much.

People were shot, execution style, right in front of him and he couldn't blink. They would kneel on the floor and beg for their lives, citing their child or wife or mother, just before the bullet drove through their skull. Young teenage girls had been rounded up and stuffed in vans destined for prostitution, a "side business" of the operation. He'd memorized the license plate of every van and sent word back to the station as soon as he could, but many still got away. The books he kept and protected showed the income from those very girls.

There were other undercover assignments, but that was the one he'd come out of anxious to see Rachel again. To know that goodness and beauty still existed in the world, only to be shut out because she was too busy.

They'd had something special.

Now he discovered it was his job that ended it? It didn't make sense.

He stared at the computer screen blindly for a few moments before finally focusing on it. A new determination grew. He and Rachel were going to have an honest talk before he was done finding out where the missing money went.

Ready to get his job done, he switched on the computer and dove into his work.

It didn't take long to come to two conclusions.

First, Rachel was an excellent business woman. Second, everything *did* balance perfectly and looked right. No adjustments had been needed going back three years. That was hard to believe, but she did say that Crystal was a whiz with numbers. And Sunnyview Ranch wasn't a huge operation. In fact, he was surprised the Oteros even bothered to buy from her, but the Oteros were good folk and if any of them had known David Henderson, Rachel's dad, they would definitely help her out.

He could go back more years, but his gut told him the answer would be found in what he'd already pulled. Next, he'd spot check the checking account balances on various days and see if they matched. Plus, he wanted more information on the CR Seed and Grain Company. They seemed to be the biggest supplier to Sunnyview.

He'd just clicked onto the bank website when the smell of freshly baked cookies wafted into the office. Hell, they smelled better than the buttermilk biscuits they served at the diner next to his apartment outside Austin. He forced himself to log in and pull up the checking account, the one with insufficient funds. He could see the deposit Rachel made to cover the bills that hadn't been paid due to the low balance. He tried to focus on the last couple transactions before that, but the cookie smell had his stomach rumbling. Crap, he should have eaten lunch.

Unable to resist, he logged off and headed out of the office. As he followed the scent of cookies, his stomach rumbled louder. He stepped into the kitchen and one word flashed through his mind. *Home.*

Sunlight streamed in through the row of windows parallel to the kitchen table as well as in the window above the sink. It lit up the counter where a bowl full of cookie dough sat, a large spoon inside leaning against the edge. To the left was the stove with cookie racks on its smooth surface filled with warm cookies and below that was Rachel's ass as she bent over to check on the batch inside the oven.

He clamped down his teeth to keep the low whistle inside. She thought that part of her anatomy was too big, but he found it perfect. With her busy below, he quietly moved forward and plucked a cookie from the racks. As he bit in, he moaned, unable to keep the sound of his enjoyment from escaping.

Rachel straightened and spun around. "Vince Gallagher, what are you doing?"

He finished chewing and swallowed, savoring every flavor before giving her a grin. "Eating one of your heart-melting cookies. These are your Mom's monster cookies, aren't they?"

Her brows lifted in surprise. "You remember what type of cookie that is?"

He nodded, having filled his mouth with the rest of the treat, enjoying the full flavor of oatmeal, chocolate, cinnamon, and walnuts. He remembered everything about them…and her.

Her face softened, but her hand went to her hip. "I'm making those for the men."

He lifted his hands to the sides. "I'm a man." He expected a sarcastic retort, but instead her gaze swept from his face down his body and back up to his crotch, and hell if his cock didn't start to harden. "If you're in doubt, I'd be happy to prove it to you."

Her head snapped up at that. "No, I'm well aware that you're a man, but I was making them for my ranch hands."

Vince took the two steps that would bring him within kissing distance. "I can be whatever kind of man you need me to be if…" He paused, noticing the sudden intake of breath through her lips. He reached around her and snagged another cookie. "I can have another."

He popped the entire treat into his mouth, chewing and grinning. He didn't care if he was acting the fool. He was in this cozy kitchen with a hot woman and a delicious cookie on his tongue.

He stilled, waiting for her wrath, but then she reached up and brushed the side of his lip.

"You have a crumb on your face."

He caught her hand and kissed her finger. "Rae, we need—"

She pulled her hand out of his grasp and turned her back. "If you're done stealing my cookies, I need to get this next batch ready."

He watched her for a moment as she scooped the dough by spoon and dropped it onto the baking sheet. He wanted to wrap his arms around her and nuzzle her neck to hear her squeal. That was her ticklish spot.

But her stance said to back off.

So he stepped around her and filched one more cookie before returning to the den.

Rachel continued to scoop the dough onto the sheet until she heard the telltale crackle of Vince's body settling into her dad's leather chair. She let out her breath and her shoulders sagged. It took her a moment to focus on the batter. She'd scooped far too many spoonfuls onto the sheet. If she put it in that way, she'd have one big cookie. It would truly be a monster cookie then.

Her lips quirked at the thought even as she rolled some of the balls of dough back onto the spoon and into the bowl then wiped the spaces clean. This was exactly what she'd been afraid of the moment she saw Vince again. She couldn't think straight when he was near.

She just hoped he and Hunter figured out her money issue fast. She had some big bills due next week. She'd remind Sam again to call the Oteros and see when they wanted their cattle delivered. It could serve as a reminder of their order and help her with her current cash flow issues.

She opened the oven, pulled out the tray of cookies and set them on the cooling racks before sliding the next dough covered cookie sheet into the oven. Glancing at the clock, she leaned her butt against one of the chairs placed at the kitchen table.

"Oh, what the heck." She picked up one of the hot cookies and took a small bite. The melted chocolate nearly burned her tongue, but the flavor was perfect, thanks to her mom's recipe. She missed her mom. She'd always been able to talk to her, even about Vince.

When he started to say they needed to talk, she thought she'd have her first ever panic attack. She could barely think when he was near, and he wanted to talk? She had plenty of questions for him such as, was his work for the Oteros dangerous like when he was with the department, or was he still with the department and did that on the side? And did he have a girlfriend?

Ugh, she couldn't start thinking like that. She finished chewing the rest of her cookie and pushed away from the table. Wiping down an empty cookie sheet, she placed it on the counter and stilled.

Why not? Why not see if there was anything still between them? "That's a dumb question."

At the creak of a floorboard beneath the leather chair in the den, she lowered her voice. "Of course there's something there. Shit, there was enough heat to bake the cookies with."

She put down the spoon. She was in a different place in her life. If she could get the ranch back on stable footing, then maybe they could pursue something. That was if he no longer went undercover for months and if he didn't hate her for breaking it off and if he didn't have a girlfriend. That was too many "ifs."

She picked up the spoon and started scooping. When she finished with that sheet, she piled cooled cookies into a plastic container. Her mom used to do the same thing for the hands.

She remembered the first time Vince had received cookies while out with her dad, herding the cattle. His appreciation had been so sincere it brought tears to her eyes. It reminded her he'd never had a mom to bake for him. That he'd turned out so well was more due to his own personality than his foster mothers.

Vince never complained about his foster parents, all four sets, but it was clear that while he'd been taken care of, he hadn't been loved. Rachel had wanted to make up for that and then just like his foster parents, she'd pushed him away. "I should call myself the foster girlfriend."

At the sound of her voice, she stilled and listened. She could just make out the sound of Vince's large fingers tapping on the keyboard. Maybe he could find the mistake quickly. Then she wouldn't have to worry about what he thought of her. She could bring him another cookie or two, but that was just asking for more heartache.

Instead, she closed the plastic container, grabbed a roll of paper towels and put them on top. She'd throw those in her saddle bag.

She'd just pulled the next batch of cookies out of the oven and placed them on cooling racks when her phone rang. Sam's name was on the display. "No, the cookies aren't ready yet." She grinned.

"You need to come out here. We have a problem."

Her gut tightened. "Did one of the men get hurt?" It was her biggest fear running the ranch.

"No, the men are fine, but the cattle aren't."

"What? What do you mean?"

There was silence on the other end of the phone, and she could hear one of her men swearing in the background. "Some are missing out of the west pasture.

You'll want to see this." Sam hung up and she stared at her phone for a second before her brain kicked in.

She shut off the oven and grabbed her hat. As she started out of the kitchen and headed toward the front of the house, she remembered Vince. "I have to meet up with Sam. I'll be back."

She threw open the screen door and jogged down the steps. Had the cattle broken through the fencing? Did they have a new predator? She dismissed her second thought. Cattle, as in more than one, wouldn't be "missing" if it was a predator. There'd be a trail to follow, a carcass to find.

As she saddled Foxglove, she picked apart every word Sam said. That he'd hung up meant she needed to come quickly. It was a habit he had when he was upset. Once her prized quarter horse was ready to go, she mounted and guided him out of the barn.

Vince stood on the front porch.

She waved as if nothing was wrong and kicked Foxglove into a gallop. She didn't need Vince to think she had an emergency or that she couldn't handle the ranch on her own. She could. She just couldn't think when he was around.

As she galloped out to the west pasture, her mind cleared. It always did while riding her horse. The two of them went back a few years. She'd stumbled upon a horse auction that had not been well advertised. She stopped to get gas on her way back from Austin where she'd gone to see Crystal when she first landed her accounting job.

There were hardly any cars at the auction barns next to the gas station, so she drove over to see what they had. The minute she'd seen the blue roan quarter horse, she knew she had to have him, but she'd never bought at auction because the prices tended to go too high for her bank account. One look into Foxglove's distrustful gaze and she had to try. After registering, she sat in one of the many empty chairs and waited.

When he was brought up, there were a few half-hearted bids, but nothing to keep her from buying him. She was shocked. Even she could see he was of good stock and his color alone made him special. The only hurdle was they required cash payment.

It had taken all her self-control not to bid against herself in her excitement. Once the auctioneer said "sold," she was out of her seat and on her phone to Crystal and Sam, Crystal to bring the cash and Sam to bring the trailer.

Her first meeting with Foxglove didn't go well. She also learned in the paperwork how he got his name. He was born in a field in the middle of a patch of Foxglove. From the notes, she could tell whoever had owned him didn't know much about horses. She wasn't sure, but she had a feeling his training had been harsh. It took her about a month to get him to accept her. Now they were inseparable.

She swore he could tell she was anxious because she barely needed to guide him in the direction she needed to go. As she crested the small hill at the beginning of the pasture, she could see Sam and three other men near the fence line. Shit, the fence line had broken. The cattle must have wandered out.

As she rode closer, she could see it was no normal break. Deep ruts left by truck tires clearly marked the route her cattle might have disappeared to. Fury threatened to overtake her, but she was the boss and if there was one thing ranch hands couldn't stomach, it was an emotional female rancher.

Slowing Foxglove, she brought him to a stop, but didn't dismount.

Sam walked over to her. "As you can see, this was intentional." Even with his hat shading his eyes, she could see her own anger reflected in his grey eyes.

"Obviously. Have you been able to figure out how many they took?"

His jaw tightened. "Yes." The word was ground out between gritted teeth. "Just one."

She knit her brow in confusion. "One cow? Was it a prank?"

Sam shook his head. "These fellers knew exactly what they came for. They took Matterhorn."

She sucked in her breath. "Shit." Matterhorn was her prize bull. Many ranchers used his semen to impregnate their cows. Besides the ranch house itself, he was her most valuable asset followed closely by her own horse. This was the last thing she needed.

"You want me to call the sheriff?" Sam looked at her expectantly.

She bit down on her automatic response. She had one former police officer in Hunter and one detective with Vince involved in her business already. Her gut told her they would want to make the next move.

As much as she hated to involve Hunter and Vince, she could already hear the dressing down she'd receive if they got wind she'd handled this on her own when they were nearby. "I'll do it. We still have extra fencing in the shed off the barn, right?"

He nodded. "Yeah, there should be enough as long as no one decides to cut any more fencing."

"I'll have Crystal order more just in case, but I doubt they'll come back. They got the best. Why bother with any others?"

"I'm sorry, Miss Rachel."

Sam's anger had to be dissipating if he was back to calling her "Miss Rachel." "It wasn't your fault. When do you think it happened?"

He tipped his Stetson up and wiped the sweat off his forehead with his bandana then resettled his hat. "It had to be last night. I had the men ride the line yesterday and everything was intact."

"We can't be out here twenty-four seven. Guess I'm going to have to invest in some of those motion cameras Crystal is always trying to get me to buy."

"Pardon me saying, but you shouldn't need any damn cameras." Sam's voice had lowered to almost a growl.

She watched her men as they herded the few curious herefords away from the opening. "No, I shouldn't, but things have changed."

Sam just shook his head. "I'll get the men started on the fence repair. It should be done by dinner time."

"Thank you."

Her foreman tipped his hat and strode off to give

instructions. She rode over to the break and looked at the tire tracks. It had to be one heavy-duty truck to get up to this pasture, through the conservation land her ranch bordered, then to return with a bull weighing over a ton in the back. She looked for trailer tracks, careful to keep Foxglove from stepping near the ruts.

There were no other tracks which meant someone loaded Matterhorn into the bed of a pick-up. That was just crazy.

She turned her horse back the way they'd come and let him pick his own pace. Maybe there was a reason Vince was in her life at the moment. If she suffered a few heart palpitations and a couple hot dreams so he could help her discover who was undercutting her operation, she'd just have to grin and bear it.

As she rode closer to the house, she could see Vince's truck was gone. She ignored the disappointment that swept through her and focused on bringing Foxglove into the barn and taking his saddle off. "You're still the most dependable male in my life, sweetie."

She set him loose into the corral and leaned on the fence for a few minutes watching him drink from the trough. His black coat interspersed with the white hair that declared him a true roan gave him a greyish color. His black legs and mane just made him that much more handsome, though not the heart-stopping handsome that a certain detective was. "At least now I can tell Vince about the loss of my bull over the phone instead of in person. Shit, I'm such a wuss."

"Oh no, I forgot about the cookies." Foxglove barely glanced at her as she spun away and strode across the hard-packed front yard. She needed to throw out the left over dough and bring the cookies out to the men. They'd be doubly appreciative after they repaired that fencing.

She let the screen door slam behind her and headed into the kitchen. When she stepped in, she froze. The leftover dough had been made into cookies and the mess of dirty dishes and cookie sheets had disappeared. There was a note on the plate of cookies.

Rae, I'll see you tomorrow. Following up on a couple possibilities. Call if you need me.

Vince's card was stapled to the bottom. It wasn't from the Austin police department. It was a simple card with his name, phone number and a cowboy hat in the corner.

She looked from the note to the clean kitchen to the baked cookies and back. Pulling out a chair, she plopped into it. He baked and cleaned too? Her heart swelled at his thoughtfulness. "Shit, I'm such a lost cause."

Chapter Four

Vince took a sip of his beer as he watched the door of Big Joe's Bar and Grill. There was no one called Big Joe associated with the bar. In fact, it was owned by an old friend of his, Bonnie. She had chosen the name to attract male customers and it worked. At least there was a grill in the kitchen, though he'd never eaten in the place.

"Looking for someone?"

Vince started as Hunter settled into the seat across from him.

"How the hell do you do that? You were always quiet, but that's inhuman."

His friend shrugged. "A few months in Afghanistan and you'd learn to walk silently, too. I take it that wasn't a requirement for undercover work?"

"No. My specialty was pretending to be someone I wasn't."

Hunter raised his brow. "Do you still get carded?"

He chuckled. "On occasion, but I think that's just the cute grocery clerk's way of checking me out. How many thirty three-year-olds do you know get carded?"

"My point exactly." Hunter looked doubtful. "You *can* grow a beard, right?"

This time he laughed. It was an old routine for the two of them. Hunter joked about his young appearance, and he pretended it had to do with all the women wanting him. There was only one woman he was focused on now, and he would work on that tomorrow. "Gotta shave every day."

The waitress came over and Hunter ordered a ginger ale.

It didn't take rocket science to figure out why. The man's wife was killed by a drunk driver. Vince kicked himself. He should have had them meet somewhere else.

He just wasn't keen on the bistro atmosphere of the two other eating establishments in Daisy Creek and the diner was only open for breakfast and lunch. "You okay with me having a beer?"

Hunter shrugged it off. "I'm not your mother."

"And I can't tell you what a relief that is. You'd make an ugly woman."

Hunter's lips quirked up on one side. "I'll take that as a compliment."

The waitress brought Hunter his drink and gave him a wink then sashayed back to the bar.

Vince wasn't surprised by Hunter's lack of interest. His friend was like himself. A one woman man. "So what did you find at the fence break. Wish I could have been there by nightfall."

"There wasn't a lot to see. Whoever stole her bull obviously just came for him and the idiots loaded him into the bed of a large pick-up truck."

He shook his head. "That's what she said. What about tire tracks?"

"I made the impressions you wanted. I followed the tracks down through the reserve and to the paved road. Luckily, there was so much dirt and mud stuck in the tires that I could track it all the way to West Highway 290. They were headed toward Austin."

Vince sat back as his mind spun. The bull incident and the missing money didn't seem connected, but they had to be. He didn't believe in coincidence. Financial ruin came to mind. As much as he was upset with Rachel, he didn't want to see her lose the ranch because someone decided she'd be easy pickings. Maybe a developer wanted the land. He'd look into that.

Hunter studied him. "Did you find anything going through Rachel's books?"

"Yes, a lot."

"Really?" Hunter took a swig of ginger ale. "I knew you were the right one for this case."

Vince pointed to an invisible spot on the table. "At first, everything looked perfect, but it was too perfect. There were no adjustments or mistakes of any kind. In three years, that's almost impossible."

"True, but Crystal *is* supposed to be a whiz at numbers."

He moved his finger to another spot on the table. "I compared the bank statements to the books." He moved his finger back to its original spot. "Even that looked right. So I decided to spot check daily balances."

"And…"

He slapped his hand down. "They didn't match. The statements and online daily balances were completely off, by thousands."

Hunter folded his arms. "How can that be?"

Vince thought about his conclusions. Two he liked and one he didn't. "Based on the discrepancy, I can rule out the accountant."

"Okay, that doesn't surprise me. From what I discovered today, she's as clean as a whistle."

He nodded. "She only has the books in her possession for a month and this problem is year-round."

Hunter whistled low between his teeth. "Are you saying Rache is lucky she still has the ranch?"

"Not necessarily. It's almost as if someone has been using her checking account for short term loans. By the end of the month, she is always solvent."

Hunter lowered his brow. "I'm not a financial whiz like you, so explain how she was suddenly short of cash in laymen's terms."

"The borrower didn't pay the money back in time."

"And the borrower is?"

"One of three people." He shrugged. "Or as best I can tell right now. It's either Sam, his wife Marie or Crystal."

Hunter stiffened. "Whoa, I don't like any of those choices. Can you suggest another?"

He shook his head. "Just Rachel's mysterious hacker theory, but I don't think she's been hacked."

"Fine, then I'll hope it's Sam or his wife. What do you need me to do next?"

"I'm with you." He thought for a moment, choosing his words carefully. "I'm going to do more online digging on all three, but I'd like you to check out an address." He pulled his wallet out of his back pocket and took a piece of paper from it. "Here it is. Find out everything you can about it."

Hunter stared at the address to the CR Seed and Grain Company then put it in his back pocket. "What is it for?"

"It's one of the companies Rachel does business with." He purposefully kept the amount of business to himself. It was a long shot, but if the other three didn't pan out, this company could be a clue.

"Anything else?"

"Yeah. Sam's wife works part-time at First Austin Bank. That's where Rachel's account is. That's too much of a coincidence for me. I'd like you to keep her in your sights tomorrow."

"Sure. What about Sam and Crystal?"

"I'm going to do more computer research on them. Maybe you could see who Crystal hangs out with tomorrow night. I'm guessing Sam's wife will be home with him and his daughter, Eva, so that will leave you free to track Crystal down. She's going to Seventh Heaven on Sandy River Road."

Hunter rubbed the condensation on his glass with

his thumb. "I'm guessing you figured that out on the computer as well."

He nodded.

"I hate night clubs." Hunter frowned.

"I'd do it, but if Crystal sees me there, she's going to wonder. If she sees you there, she'll just think you were having a night out on the town. Besides, in black, no one will see you."

Hunter shook his head. "And where will you be tomorrow night?"

"I need to ask Rachel some tough questions."

"About the missing money or about you and her?"

Vince took a swallow of beer. "That obvious?"

"Fuck yeah."

Hell. He tipped his hat up and brought it back into place. "She told me today she'd broken off our relationship seven years ago because of my job. That's not what she said to me back then."

Hunter frowned. "Damn, that sucks."

"Yeah. That she lied to me has me pissed off, but since my job has changed—I'm thinking a lot."

Hunter took a sip of ginger ale, but didn't say anything.

Vince knew the tactic was to make a perp talk. He was no perp, but he didn't mind talking, at least not to Hunter. The guy was a vault when it came to secrets, never mind a friend's conversation. "We had something growing between us. We even talked about what it was like for the wife of a cop. She didn't appear to be concerned. I thought it was because she had confidence that I could keep myself alive."

"And now you're wondering if it was because she didn't see herself as an officer's wife."

He nodded. "Her father died while I was undercover. I didn't come up for air for over six months."

"Shit, that's a long time." Hunter looked askance at him. "You saw shit that woke you up at night."

"Yeah." The vision of an overweight man on his knees begging for a second chance rushed before his eyes. He jerked at the remembered gunshot to the man's forehead. He took a gulp of beer, ignoring the sweat that trickled down his back at the memory.

"Rachel was an angel by that time and you couldn't wait to see her." Hunter wasn't even looking at him.

Hell, it was similar to what Hunter had gone through overseas, only his wife died. At least Rachel was still alive. "Forget I mentioned it."

Hunter's gaze snapped to him. "No, keep talking. That's what my therapists always said. I didn't believe them until I started talking to the right person."

"Right person?"

A smirk formed on Hunter's face. "Adriana."

Vince shook his head, but understanding dawned. "You think I should tell all this to Rachel."

Hunter just looked at him over his glass, his meaning clear.

"First, I have to corner her. That woman does not want to talk. Second, I'm not sure she's the one I should talk to. The only reason I'm in her life right now is because you brought me in. We are done as she reminded me today."

Hunter shrugged. "You'll be at the ranch all day

tomorrow." Then he pushed back his chair and stood. "Speaking of the ranch, I better show my face or Rachel will start worrying."

"Right. Thanks for the advice."

Hunter stared at him a minute. "We go back and I like you, but Rachel and I go back farther. Don't break her heart and make me come after you."

Vince stood, throwing down a few bills to cover their tab. "Believe me, you don't have to worry about that. It's my heart that's been beat up and spit out. She's the one who made the break. I'd be a glutton for punishment if I tried to fix it."

"Honestly, I agree with you."

They walked toward the door together, the locals watching as they left. Vince had a feeling that by tomorrow morning, everyone would know they had returned to Daisy Creek. He just hoped that didn't hurt their investigation. Then again, both being from the area would make it look like a reunion.

Did Rachel see it that way?

~~~~~

Rachel rode into the barn, tired from a long day of work. Her shirt was filthy and sweat trickled down between her breasts, making her bra itch. Sam had called to say he needed to stay home with Eva who had a fever, so she'd ridden out with her men.

She hoped Eva wasn't too sick. The poor girl seemed to attract illnesses and broken bones like flowers attracted bees.

Dismounting from Foxglove, she unsaddled him and brought him to the cleaning station. Picking up the curry comb, she started to brush him down when her gaze landed on Vince's truck.

Shit, she'd hoped he'd be gone by now. How could a man find out so much about people simply by using a computer? What happened to chasing down the bad guys and breaking into their homes with a warrant? Shouldn't he be tailing her hacker or something?

Foxglove looked back at her.

"Sorry, sweetie. Was I a little too rough?"

He stared at her a moment longer then faced forward again.

She patted him. "See, that's what happens when I have Vince on my mind. I can't concentrate on anything."

She managed to focus on Foxglove for a few more minutes before her mind wandered again. Not everything about Vince bothered her. In fact, that was the problem. There was too much about him that she loved.

Between his hard toned body, good heart, and intelligence, she was overwhelmed by him. She simply had no defense against him. "It's only been twenty-four hours since that man walked back into my life and already I'm tripping over my own thoughts."

She forced herself to be gentle. It wasn't Foxglove's problem that she ruined her only chance at real love. "Vince doesn't appear to be angry with me." She snorted. "But he's a cowboy and he'd be polite no matter what. I don't want polite. I want him to get angry or just take me in his arms and kiss me already." She froze and looked around the barn.

She relaxed when she confirmed she was alone. "Yeah, like you've given him any time to get near you." She moved to the other side of Foxglove, just the sound of her own voice helping her sift through her thoughts. "What are you afraid of, Rae? That he'll say no way, Jose? You broke my heart once, why would I let you in again?"

She brushed along her horse's back. "You know what I think, Foxglove? I think he's more man than I am." Ah shit, listen to her now. That had to be one of the stupidest statements she'd made in years. Vince really did mess up her brain.

She needed to think about something entirely different like the fact that no new breaks had appeared in the fences or that Crystal had called that morning to make sure she was okay. Her sister's anger over the lost bull did make her feel better. The fact that Crystal said she'd get on the phone with the insurance company was also a relief.

When the Sheriff came over yesterday after Vince called him, Rachel had the feeling he wasn't really listening. Either Vince had told him all the particulars, or he wasn't that concerned. He seemed overly confident they would find her bull.

She chuckled. All they had to do is look for a messed up pick-up truck to figure out who took Matterhorn. It wasn't as if her bull was docile or anything.

She finished rubbing down Foxglove then moved him into his stall. She gave him his feed and snatched an apple from a basket she had on a shelf nearby. "Here you go, sweetie. I'm sorry I was too rough."

Foxglove took the offered treat between his teeth and moved toward his feed, chewing as he went.

She closed the stall door and leaned against it. There was no more avoiding the inevitable. She had to go into the house. She stared unseeing at the stall across the way, the light in the barn was low as the open barn doors faced eastward and the sun was far west now.

As she focused, her pulse increased. The memory of her and Vince making love in that stall hit her clear and hot. They'd come in from a ride and he lifted her off her horse. It was Honey back then, her old Palomino.

His touch had been possessive and anxious, but they'd taken care of their mounts first. Then he'd literally swept her off her feet and pulled her into the stall. In their haste to get their clothes off, she'd tripped and fallen into him. He'd been standing on one leg to toe-off his boot and they went down together, him cushioning her from the prickly straw.

They laughed before they kissed and because they hadn't even grabbed a blanket, he lay beneath her, his bare butt on his shirt giving her a place for her knees as she rode him. They'd come together, his mouth catching her moans of pleasure so her parents wouldn't hear.

She shook her head to dispel the image, but her body remembered. "Great. Now I get to walk in the house hornier than a cottontail and try to resist the man."

She pushed away from Foxglove's stall, unbuckled her chaps and hung them on a peg outside the tack room. She strode toward the house. What she needed was a cold shower. What her body wanted was a hot bath. What her heart wanted was her bed, with Vince in it.

Frustrated, she stomped up the porch steps and opened the screen door and front door. As soon as she stepped inside, she slowed as the coolness of the air conditioning hit her. After riding hard all day, something she rarely had to do anymore, the temperature of the house refreshed her.

She closed the door then headed for the kitchen. The scent of beef stew wafted by. She hadn't seen Crystal's car out there. Vince wasn't cooking, was he?

Stepping into the kitchen, she halted. Lord have mercy! Vince stood at her stove in a red checkered shirt and tight blue jeans that hugged his ass beautifully. He was in the process of lifting a wooden spoon to his lips and tasting its contents.

The need to taste his lips rose hard. She grabbed the door frame to keep herself in place.

"I ran a bath for you." Vince turned and faced her, a small smile on his lips. "After a day of riding, I thought you might enjoy one." His gaze moved from her face, to her dirty shirt, to her jeans and dust covered boots.

Oh shit. Her body responded to his look like a mare in heat. Her clothes were suddenly too confining and she took a step forward as if propelled by instinct. She wrapped her arms around her waist to keep herself from moving closer. "Thank you."

She should say more, but her mouth didn't want to

work. Neither did her legs as she told them to back away. Luckily, her stomach rumbled, letting them both know she was hungry. She flushed and pointed behind her. "I'll head upstairs now."

Tearing her gaze from his smiling eyes, she turned on her heel and practically ran out of the room to the stairs. She took the steps two at a time, anxious to put space between her and Vince. She was in big trouble. She just couldn't think with him around.

She made it to her bedroom, which had once been her parents'. It now sported lavender walls and deep purple bedding, very different from her mother's white and pink. She dropped her hat on her dresser and stripped as she walked, unable to get her clothes off fast enough. Leaving a trail behind her, she opened the door to the master bath and sighed.

Closing the bathroom door with one hand, she tugged the elastic from her braid with the other. The beige colored soaking tub was full of bubbles, and the lavender scent she loved filled the room.

She didn't even put her hair up, too weary and too tempted by the bath waiting for her to care. Besides, it needed washing too.

She tested the water with her hand. It was warm, not too hot, and perfect for a soak. Stepping in, she lowered herself into the bubbles with a loud moan of contentment.

"I could get used to this."

She closed her eyes and let the water soothe her aching muscles. If Vince hoped to sway her with kindness, he needn't have bothered. She already knew how kind he was, but she sure as heck didn't mind.

Slipping under the water, she wet her hair then pulled herself up to rest her arms on the indents of the tub. Her mom had insisted on the large tub, saying she wanted to pamper herself once in a while, but Rachel knew her mother bought such a large one so her father could use it. And he had.

Would Vince like it, now that he'd seen it? She opened her eyes and scanned the room. He had to go through her bedroom to get to this bathroom. What had he seen? Frantically, she tried to remember if she'd left underwear on the floor or made her bed.

She groaned and closed her eyes. No, she hadn't made her bed and she was ninety-percent sure there were clothes on her floor when she'd left to ride out this morning. "Well, too bad. That's just who I am. The man probably thinks he dodged a bullet when I broke it off with him. Good. That means he shouldn't be mad at me then."

At that thought, her heart squeezed. She definitely still loved him. The question was, did she love the man she remembered or the man he was now?

"I brought you some blackberries to hold you over until dinner." Vince's voice, so close to her ear, had her eyes popping open.

CHAPTER FIVE

Rachel covered her breasts with her arms, but it didn't matter, the bubbles did a good job of hiding her naked body. "What are you doing in here?"

He settled his fine ass on the side of the tub. "We need to talk."

"What? Now? I'm kind of busy." She brought her hand out of the water to gesture to the bubbles.

"You're always busy. This is the only way I could think of to keep you in one place long enough for us to settle a few things."

She'd never thought of him as underhanded, but she should have. He was an undercover detective. He always had to be one step ahead. Shit, he was leap years ahead of her. "Fine. So talk."

He shook his head. "No, *we* need to talk. First though, you need some blackberries or your stomach will be drowning out our words."

She felt the heat rise in her cheeks again. Her mom

had always said it was unladylike for a woman's body to make noise. "Where'd you get the blackberries?"

He shrugged. "From the west side of the house. Your bushes are full of them."

She'd completely forgotten the blackberries were ripe. She needed to add that to her growing list of things to do tomorrow.

"Open your mouth." Vince held a single blackberry in front of her.

She lifted her right hand from the water again. "I can feed myself."

"With lavender water? No, open your mouth."

She stared into his brown eyes and gave up. The man could be more stubborn than Matterhorn. Now might be a good time to find out what he'd discovered about her bull. She opened her mouth and he popped the berry in. The sweet tartness of the fruit splashed across her tongue as she bit down on it.

Wow, she'd forgotten how good the first berries of the season tasted. When she finished chewing, he held another berry before her.

Giving him a disgruntled look that he had to feed her, she opened her mouth again.

This time he slid the berry in, his fingertips touching her lips. The scent of beef stew broke through the lavender cloud as she closed her mouth, suddenly aware of the motion of her lips as he stared at them.

There was a tension in Vince's face that she remembered. It was the look he had when his body reacted to hers. Was that how he looked at other women as well? She glanced at his hands. There was no ring of any kind, but since he went undercover that may not mean anything.

Before he could feed her another berry, she turned her head and spoke. "Are you married?"

His brows rose. "No." He pushed another berry between her lips.

Subtle she wasn't. Didn't he want to know if she had someone in her life? Maybe he didn't care. She watched his eyes. He may not care about her, but he was definitely attracted to her.

Vince held another berry in front of her. She opened her mouth and this time as he slid it in, she purposefully closed her lips around his fingers.

Was that a sudden tension she saw in his jaw? Knowing she could affect him as much as he affected her had her feeling a bit more at ease.

He slipped another berry into her mouth, his gaze not leaving her lips. "You never told me it was my job you couldn't handle. Why didn't you?"

His eyes were so intense, it took her brain a minute to override the heat in her body. "I didn't want you to have to choose between me and your job. Besides, it wasn't just that. I told you the truth. I just couldn't divide myself that many ways. Dad's death meant I had to run the ranch and then Mom was diagnosed with cancer and Crystal was suspended from school for drugs. I couldn't even handle that. I had to get Crystal to a therapist because I didn't have the time she needed in order to help her."

Vince's face changed as he put the bowl of berries aside. "I told you I could help."

"I know." Her need to make him understand without hurting him more had her softening her voice. "But your time wasn't your own. Your department needed you and one day I might be able to depend on you but the next you'd be called to go undercover and I'd be left with more to do than I expected. I wasn't at a maturity level to handle that."

His face had become hard and a spot near his jaw twitched. "If you told me that, I could have made arrangements."

She sighed. "And those arrangements might be you leaving the force and the work you loved."

"Loved?" His voice was harsh. "Sure, getting the bad guys was a rush, but the number of innocents I saw killed or forced into prostitution or shot up with drugs… it felt like a losing battle." The tic in his cheek became more pronounced. "All I wanted was to come home from the job to something good and untarnished."

Her heart constricted at his words. "I didn't know."

"No, you didn't. And I would have never told you." His gaze moved above her head as if he'd forgotten he spoke to her. "I would have protected you from all the scum and ugliness I saw every day. The stabbing of men accused of being disloyal, the children that ran drugs, the women raped for the fun of it." His eyes reconnected with hers. "You could have erased it all."

She felt her eyes smart with tears. "I'm sorry. I wasn't strong enough."

He bent forward and took her shoulders in his hands. "You were strong, are strong. That's why I loved you."

At his declaration, her stomach tightened around the berries and threatened to eject them all. Her throat restricted her voice to the point she could only whisper. "I loved you, too."

Vince gazed into her eyes as if he would look into her soul. Then, without warning, he pulled her up against his chest and kissed her.

It wasn't the gentle kisses he'd given her in the past. This was raw hunger and hurt and pain.

She grasped him around the waist and opened for him, letting him find solace as their tongues clashed. His need for her fired off a string of sparks and she held him tight, her wet breasts pressed against the cotton of his shirt.

Vince broke the kiss only to pull her to her feet and sweep her soaking wet, into his arms. He walked through the open door of the bathroom and placed her on the bed, his whole body covering hers as soon as her back hit her crumpled sheets.

His mouth took hers again and the fire at her core sent heat to every nerve in her body. His belt buckle pressed on her naked belly, yet she pushed her hips against his jean clad legs, wanting the clothes barrier between them gone.

She'd been fooling herself to think she did the right thing so long ago. He was the other half of her whole.

He broke their kiss, only to move lower and latch

onto her breast. His tongue swept around her areola before his teeth nibbled at her hardened tip. She clutched his head in her hands, his short hair stimulating her palms even as his shirt rubbed against the juncture of her thighs. Her entrance moistened with her desire.

She lifted one leg and wrapped it around him, trying to get closer, needing his skin against her.

"Rae," he spoke against her breast, his voice gruff with wanting. "I need you."

Her heart thudded hard in her chest, tears threatening at the silent plea in his voice. "Come to me."

Vince pulled himself back until he stood. Reaching into his back pocket, he took out a condom and ripped it open with his teeth as he unbuckled his pants with his other hand. Unzipping his jeans, he lowered them and his underwear just enough to release his full package.

He pressed the condom on his tip and looked at her as he rolled it on. "I can't wait."

Her sheath flooded at his words. She lifted her arms.

With a groan he lay over her again then lifted his hips to position his hard tip at her opening. His hands held her head and as his mouth descended toward hers, his cock entered her.

Rachel wrapped her arms around Vince, pulling him closer, lifting her hips to fully encase him inside her. She welcomed him home with her body and her heart. She sucked on his tongue inside her mouth as her sheath tightened around him.

Vince moved away and she whimpered as he left

her. But he drove himself into her again, pushing her into the bed as he thrust to the hilt and held her there.

His mouth left hers to kiss her chin, her neck, her shoulder even as his hips pulled back again and he pushed into her, sliding against the pleasure points within her.

"Yes." His roughened voice whistled through her like an aphrodisiac, rebounding through her brain and into her heart. His mouth found her breast again and he sucked gently, lightly tugging at her nipple as he pulled himself out, only to let go her breast as he thrust home again.

She burrowed her hands beneath his shirt, desperate to feel his skin. Her right hand brushed over two bumps before she kneaded her fingers into the hard muscles of his back. The feel of his strength as his muscles bunched and moved with his thrusts made her feel small beneath him.

Every thrust pushed her closer to her climax. The rocking of his clothed body against her naked skin, sensitized her from the outside while inside his cock sent bursts of pleasure that spread throughout her.

Vince needed her and she let him take her. He groaned as his movements sped up, becoming shorter, until he did no more than rub against her, stroking her clit as his cock buried deep inside her, pressing her farther into the mattress.

This is what he had wanted for them, this coming together in the most natural of ways. This connection that could heal and cleanse and wrap them in goodness. But she'd denied them. Denied him.

Her moans became quick pants, short high vocal noises, cuing him into her growing pleasure. He pushed hard into her tight sheath, loving how tightly she held him and sucked at him as he pulled away slightly.

He couldn't get enough. It was as if he would take all she had to make up for the years they'd been apart, but that was impossible. Even as his balls tightened in readiness, his resentment grew. He rubbed himself against her clit, pushing into her, wanting to punish and pleasure at the same time.

Her fingers bit into his back as she arched with her orgasm, her yell triggering his own.

He grasped her tight, his release flowing into the condom as she spasmed around him. He groaned in pleasure—triumph and irritation rumbling through him.

She stroked her hands down his back as his breathing evened out. She'd given him some of what she'd kept from him over all these years.

Peace.

He lifted his head and looked at her.

She smiled, her blue eyes soft with his loving.

His mind jerked against his thought. He couldn't love her again. "I better get some food into you." He pulled his hips back, easing out of her.

She sucked in her breath, her brow knit with disappointment.

Turning toward the bathroom, he strode in and closed the door. Hell, what a mess he was. He'd thought he knew what he wanted, but he didn't. Somewhere in the back of his mind, he thought having sex with Rachel would make everything go away, but now it was worse.

He disposed of the condom and washed up. Somewhere in his mixed up head was the notion that to feel human again, to feel that there was good in the world, all he needed to do was to make love to Rachel. But his resentment tripped him up and grew with their intimacy. It blocked his love and left him frustrated.

He came back out, his jeans pulled up, his belt buckled and his shirt tucked into his pants. "I'll get dinner served. Don't take too long or your stomach will be rumbling again." He strode toward the door. When he reached it, he turned.

Now he should say how good it felt to be with her again, but it didn't. "Don't be late." With that, he headed for the stairs, his cowboy boots loud on the steps.

He strode into the kitchen and pulled out two large bowls. What the hell was he doing? He'd just had sex with the woman he'd always loved despite a bellyful of resentment poisoning his insides.

She'd soothed his soul but sent it reeling off into another direction.

He pulled a ladle out of a drawer. All these years they could have been together, if she'd just told him the truth instead of trying to protect him. He could have looked for another job, one he liked. He could have helped her and she would have helped him, kept him sane.

Every time he thought of his days on the force, he felt dirty, sullied by the company he'd been forced to keep for the good of society. But he would think of her and he felt washed clean. But just now, it all merged, his feelings a jumbled mess.

He looked down at the ladle in his hand. It was bent backward. Fuck.

Honestly, I agree with you. Hunter's words came back to haunt him.

He bent the ladle back to its proper position and plopped the stew in the bowls. The creak of the floorboards above his head warned him she was up and about. He couldn't wrap his head around what he felt.

He placed the bowls on the table just as she came through the door. She'd changed into a too-big-for-her t-shirt, pajama bottoms and a pair of ratty slippers that looked like they may have been raccoons at some point. Her hair was pulled back in a simple ponytail but still pale blonde wisps escaped.

Hell, she was just as beautiful like this as she was in jeans and chaps. "Just in time." He held out a chair for her.

Her eyes widened in surprise, but she sat without saying a word.

He took the seat opposite her, waiting for her to taste the stew. He knew it was good and despite his mixed emotions for her, he wanted to see her reaction.

She blew on a spoonful and tasted it. "Oh wow. This is really good."

"Glad you like it." Satisfied, he took a mouthful and swallowed. It needed more pepper, but it would do. "Tell me what has happened over the last seven years."

She choked on her stew before wiping her mouth. "Why do you want to know?"

"Lots of reasons, but the most important is that it may have something to do with your missing money." He gave her a smile of encouragement and took another mouthful himself.

She laid down her spoon. "Let's see. After Dad died, I took care of Mom. She didn't last long. Not more than a year. I think after Dad passed, she really didn't see a point in living. They were so in love." She paused to take up her spoon again and have another mouthful.

"There were medical bills, but Dad had provided for us pretty well, as long as the ranch continued to make a profit. Of course, I had to pay for Crystal's therapist, which wasn't cheap. But I had suggested it to her and she took it upon herself to find someone she liked. That's how I knew she was willing to get help."

"Who?"

"Who was her therapist?"

He nodded.

She frowned. "It was a Dr. Feller, Fuller, something like that."

"Do you mean Fielder?" He remembered seeing that name on a number of checks.

"Yes, that's the one. She saw that woman for a couple years until she felt better. I think it was losing Dad and then Mom during that time in her life. She got into drugs and sex, even lost her baby which devastated her though she didn't really like the child's father. I can't take any credit for Crystal getting her act together except for making the suggestion that she see someone."

Vince continued to eat without making a comment. In the silence, he built a connection between what he saw in the books and the deeper research he'd done that day. He didn't like his conclusions.

Rachel finally continued. "After that, Crystal finished college. I hired Sam before that and I bought Foxglove. Matterhorn I acquired a couple years earlier. There were improvements to the house and barns, and of course, the birthing of new cows and all the usual work on a ranch."

He finally picked up the pattern he'd been missing about Rachel. "What did you do for fun?"

She paused, her spoon halfway to her mouth. "Fun?"

"Yes. Hobbies, vacations, nights out with friends, boyfriends."

She put the spoon in her mouth then swallowed. "I don't have time for hobbies or vacations. This is a small operation so my crew is lean, but knowledgeable. I need to be here. I have a few friends from high school I see once in a while and a couple from college I chat with over the phone. But honestly, by the time my day is done, a movie and a couple cookies is all I need." She smiled tentatively, almost apologetically. "I know. Not a very exciting life."

He didn't respond. The fact that Rachel never, ever put herself first became perfectly clear. Her life was all about her responsibilities to others and the ranch itself. That insight took the sting out of her lying to him in a way he couldn't have imagined. Her actions that night when she broke it off with him fit. It wasn't about him.

He studied her as his jumbled feelings settled in to a comfortable spot. If he'd looked at their relationship before with an investigative eye, he still would have missed it because there hadn't been enough evidence. Now, years later, it all made sense. That was the break he needed to finally put the pieces together. Rachel knew no other way, but that wasn't living. It was existing.

"I think we need to change that." His heart began to find some stability.

She waved her spoon in front of her. "Oh no, I'm perfectly happy with the way my life is right now. I don't need any more excitement than insufficient funds notices and a stolen bull, thank you."

Hell, where was his mind? He'd completely forgotten to ask her. "Have you told anyone about those?"

She rolled her eyes. "I think everyone from here to Austin knows about Matterhorn. That's probably why the Sheriff thought they'd find him."

He shook his head. "No, I meant the money issues."

She sat back and her shoulders slumped. "No. I didn't want anyone to know."

"What about Crystal and Sam?"

She shook her head.

"Good. Don't tell them. I don't want them to accidently slip and give our investigation away." *Or know I'm investigating them.*

She came alert at that. "You think it's someone who knows us?"

He nodded. "I do, but I'm not done following a couple trails yet. Then again, we were speaking about your lack of excitement."

She blushed. "I think I've had enough excitement for one day." She didn't look at him.

He kicked himself. He shouldn't have had sex with her when his own heart was so confused. "I didn't mean tonight. Friday night Big Joe's has a live band. Why don't we go down so you can have some fun?"

She snapped her gaze back to him and gave him a shrewd look. "Have you been talking to Crystal?"

"No. Why?"

"No reason." She crossed her arms over her waist. "I have a question for *you*."

"What?" He raised his eyebrow, curious.

"Do you still work for the police department?"

Though her words were light as if she'd run into an old friend on the street and was just catching up, he was well aware of how important his answer was. "No."

Her arms loosened. "And this job you have with the Oteros? Do you go away for long periods of time?"

He chose his words carefully, especially after the search for Aron down in Mexico. "Sometimes, but I'm not undercover, so I can usually communicate unless there is spotty cell phone coverage."

"Shit, we have that in the north pasture." She grimaced. "What about the danger? Is it like it was on the force?"

Again he thought of the fire fight down in Mexico. Hell, they'd had to make war on a drug lord complete with explosions, automatic weapons and helicopters. But it wasn't like undercover work. He didn't have to live day in and day out with the scum of the Earth. "It's a lot less dangerous."

Her arms unfolded completely, her relief obvious.

"But it does get dangerous sometimes, just in a more direct way."

"You mean like breaking down the door of a bull-napper and shooting up the place?"

He chuckled. "Yes, something like that."

She smiled, then rose and picked up their bowls. "You cooked, so I'll clean up."

"That sounds fair." He stood as well. "I have something else I want to research before calling it a day."

"Really? Do you always work so tirelessly on a case?"

"Yes. Don't you work tirelessly in your job?"

She opened her mouth then closed it. She finally responded. "Good point."

As she turned toward the sink, he strode from the room. He wanted to check on that doctor and send a message to an old friend he had who was still at the department.

As he powered up the computer, he inhaled the scent of the leather chair and listened to the clink of the dishes being rinsed and loaded into the dishwasher in the kitchen.

It reminded him of when he used to come to Sunnyview. Rachel had brought him here, but her family and even the house had embraced him, made him feel like part of the family. He'd never had that before or since.

He looked around the den, what Rachel called her office, but it was still her father's den, his pictures on the wall, his books in the bookcases. Rachel's activity in the kitchen reminded him of her mother's, of family. This could be a typical evening for him if he wanted it to be… and if Rae wanted it to be. The question was, did both of them still want it?

Chapter Six

Vince felt his phone vibrate in his back pocket. Carefully, he extracted himself from under Rachel's head, slipping a couch pillow beneath her. He didn't want to wake her. It had taken some persuasion to get her to relax on the couch with him after dinner.

Pulling out his phone, he responded to the written message and quietly stepped outside.

Walking off the porch, he made his way toward his truck where Hunter stood, his silhouette clear in the moonlight. "Tell me."

"I found out why Marie works at the First Austin Bank. Crystal put in a word with the manager of the local branch."

"How the hell did you find that out?" Vince had to admit, he was impressed.

Hunter shrugged. "I went to her teller window and asked for change for a hundred. Then I told her I'd heard from the Hendersons that this was a good bank and that

I was thinking of opening an account. She couldn't say enough about both Rachel and Crystal."

"Smart. What about Crystal's night on the town?"

Hunter tipped his head. "That depends on which night. From the sound of her friends, she's out about five nights a week and from her familiarity with the bartenders and waitresses, she's a regular. She bought three rounds for over fifteen people and she was dressed to impress."

"According to Rachel, Crystal has a very good job at one of the major accounting firms, but she supplements her income with the proceeds from the ranch."

"I didn't hear anything about her job." Hunter shrugged. "I did hear a couple of her male friends complaining. It appears that Crystal never spends more than one night with a man, so I was thinking one of her cast-offs might be pissed off enough to steal a bull."

"Interesting. But I doubt the man would borrow money from the ranch's checking account."

"You think the two issues are connected?" Hunter's doubt was obvious.

"I do. I'm just not sure how."

Hunter didn't say anything. The night was silent except for the occasional shuffle by the horses in the barn.

Vince hesitated to tell Hunter what he discovered, mainly because it wasn't good, but also because he didn't have a solid trail yet.

Hunter finally spoke again, keeping his voice low. "I checked out the address you gave me. It's one of those shared office space places where there's a receptionist for about twenty companies, all small, and they rent out meeting rooms. There are also single offices with computers in them. Some are empty, but others are being occupied."

Vince let out his breath. Hell, that wasn't what he wanted to hear even if it was the break in the case he was hoping for. "That's the address of CR Seed and Grain Company. I discovered today that it's not an actual seed company, but more of a pass through. It takes the money and somewhere it gets the supplies that are ordered."

"Sounds like a front." Hunter leaned against his rented Jeep.

"It has to be. I also found out the payments to Crystal's former therapist went to the same account."

"That doesn't make any sense."

He took a deep breath. "No, it doesn't. That leads me to Crystal or someone she knows, like maybe that therapist. But I also discovered that Sam's daughter has had an enormous amount of medical bills that started with a lung condition when she was born."

"Shit. That's financial motivation right there. So is his wife off the hook?"

He shook his head. "I figured out why the daily balances didn't match the bank statements."

Hunter waited.

"The bank statements are fake."

Hunter's brow lowered. "Wait, how can the bank send out fake bank statements?"

"They can't unless someone was switching them before they were mailed out. They are on the same paper."

"But Marie is a teller. She wouldn't have access to the bank statements. They probably come from some major bank location."

Vince silently agreed. It could be that Marie was simply supplying the paper and someone else, like Crystal, made them look real by switching them out after they arrived at the ranch and she'd opened them. That wasn't something he was ready to discuss, especially with Hunter who considered the women as close as sisters. "Why would Rachel still be getting bank statements mailed when she can go online and pull them up?"

"Good question." Hunter looked past him at the house. "Is she still awake?"

"No. She fell asleep in front of the television, so you can sneak in and she'll be none the wiser."

"So what's next, Mr. PI?

He moved his hand up to lift his hat, but he'd left it in the house. He kept coming back to the stolen bull. If it was to leave a message like the Oteros received a while back, the perps would have left part of it. His gut told him it had to do with money. "I've been off the ranch longer than you. How long do you think it'd take to sell Rachel's bull?"

"In a public or private sale?"

"Private. Very private."

Hunter thought for a moment. "If the seller already had a buyer in mind, it could be less than a day. Why, what are you thinking?"

"I'm thinking that if the bull was stolen to sell, then money will be showing up in the checking account anytime now."

"Shit, I'm glad I brought you in on this case. Give me an enemy with a gun or an overzealous Dom with a whip and I'll take care of it. This finance stuff gives me a headache."

He raised his brows. "Overzealous Dom with a whip?"

Hunter grinned. "Yup. It's how Adriana and I got together."

It sounded like something Pablo Otero could shed some light on, but Vince preferred staying in the dark on that one.

Hunter pointed to the house. "How about you walk me in. I'll be up most the night, but with the day work you have me doing, I might just fall asleep before dawn. I can't tell you how much I thought about the peace and quiet out here while in that nightclub."

Vince turned and fell into step with his friend. He wasn't tired either. In fact, his mind was buzzing with possibilities.

"So what do you want me to work on tomorrow? I have a couple people I need to visit, but I'm free mostly."

"I want to find out who took that bull."

"You and me both."

"As soon as money comes into Rachel's account, if it comes in, I'll trace the source and call you to do what you do best."

Hunter opened the screen door, but waited on the main door. "And that is?"

"Sneak up on someone."

Hunter's smile in the moonlight promised retribution. Vince was damn glad he had the man working with him and not against him.

~~~~~

Rachel stood in front of Foxglove's stall and stared. Her horse was gone. Taking her phone from her pocket, she called Sam. "Good morning, did you or one of the men saddle up Foxglove?"

"No, Miss Rachel. I thought you went for an early morning ride. He wasn't there when Jack went to feed him. Did he get out?"

She looked around the stall, but everything was locked up tight. A sinking feeling hit the bottom of her stomach and she walked out of the barn. "No, he didn't get out. He was taken."

"What? I'll be right there." Sam hung up the phone.

It was one thing to take her money and her prize bull, but to take her horse was inexcusable. If they thought insurance money would pacify her, they were dead wrong.

She carefully walked around the entrance to the barn, but her men had already been in and out a number of times. So she strode down to the yard, looking for any unfamiliar tire tracks.

She could see where Vince's truck had been last night. Hunter's rental was still there, but there were just too many tracks. She took her phone out and dialed Vince, surprised he wasn't already at the ranch. She hoped that meant he was closing in on where her missing money had gone.

It was Wednesday and Crystal would be paying those bills on Friday.

"Rachel, what is it?"

"Why do you think something's wrong?"

He paused. "Call it a gut feeling."

She could hear highway traffic in the background. "They took my horse." As she said the words, her slim hold on her emotions slipped and her throat closed.

"Foxglove is gone?"

She nodded with her phone, her tears starting for real now. "Uh-huh."

"Hell! I'm on my way. Don't touch anything and do what you can to keep the area clear."

"It's too late." Her voice shook, her frustration and heartache poured into every word.

"Rae, I promise. We'll find him. Wake up Hunter. He'll know what to do until I can get there."

She sniffed and nodded.

"Rae? Can you do that for me?"

"Yes." She wiped her eyes with her sleeve. "Get here fast."

"On my way." Vince hung up and she sniffed again.

If whoever had taken Foxglove hurt one hair on his body, she would shoot them. She strode back to the house, her little baby fit over. Letting the front door slam shut, she yelled upstairs to Hunter. "Get down here! Please!"

Stomping into the kitchen, she cut into the coffee cake she'd made earlier. Wrapping a large hunk in a paper towel, she stalked to the bottom of the stairs. She didn't care if Hunter was used to the night shift. She needed his help.

Hunter came down fast, somehow missing all the creaking boards on the stairs. She shoved the coffee cake at him. "Here. You have to do your detective thing."

He caught the coffee cake against his chest. "What happened?"

She balled her hands and ground out the words between gritted teeth. "They took my horse."

"Aw, fuck."

"Exactly. Vince is on his way, but he said you knew what to do to keep people from messing with the evidence." She turned away from him and strode toward the living room. "But all my hands have already messed things up."

She stopped in front of the gun case and pulled out her rifle. Grabbing bullets, she loaded it. When she turned around, she found Hunter watching her. "What are you waiting for? Go do your thing."

He raised one eyebrow, but didn't move. "Rache, what are you going to do with that?"

She glared at him. "I'm going to shoot someone. What else? I'm going to carry this with me until we find my horse and if my horse is fine, I may not kill the bastard. But if Foxglove has been harmed in any way, I'm going to make my own justice."

Hunter looked at her a moment longer before he turned around and headed outside.

She watched him through the window as he strode

into the barn. Good. Now where was Vince? Why wasn't he here like he'd been every morning? Maybe this was a sign that she couldn't depend on him.

She stalked outside and met Sam as he rode in, keeping him far from the barn. He tied his mount to the front porch and dismounted. "I got here at six this morning and he wasn't in his stall." He eyed the gun in her hands.

"Good, tell that to Vince and Hunter when Vince gets here. They will want to narrow down the timeframe."

"Uh, why are you carrying your rifle?"

She pinned him with her angry gaze. "Because I'm gonna shoot the son of a bitch who took my horse."

Sam took his bandana from his pocket and wiped his brow. "Do you know who that is?"

She looked away. "Not yet, but I will. Even if I have to look in every damn barn in Texas." A dust cloud in the distance announced a vehicle speeding down the dirt road toward the driveway. She ignored her foreman and strode toward it. There was no way she'd let anyone disturb the scene further. Even now Hunter was using twine to rope off the area.

The truck came to a halt just outside the fence that proclaimed it Sunnyview Ranch. As the dust cleared, Vince stepped from the truck. He started toward her, his stride confident as he stayed to the side of any tracks or footsteps.

Now that the vehicle was stopped, she could see he'd driven off road. Shit. Her anger started to drift away and her heart lurched, causing her tears to start all over again.

He reached her and enveloped her in his arms. He spoke against her hair. "I'll find him. Don't worry."

She held on until she got control of herself. She pulled her head back and looked at him. "I'm not worried." She raised the rifle in her right hand. "I'm pissed."

He grinned. "Good because so am I."

She stepped away from him, determined to stand on her own. "Do you have any ideas?"

He nodded, but his grin disappeared. "I found the person who took Matterhorn."

"Is my bull all right?"

"I think so. The person who stole Matterhorn sold him. I need Hunter to track down the buyer while I keep after the thief."

"Then go. What are you doing here?" She pushed him away.

He looked at her as if she'd lost her mind. "I thought you wanted me to find Foxglove."

She felt the heat rise in her cheeks. "Aren't they the same person?"

He tilted his cowboy hat up and put it back down. "I'm counting on it. But I need to take a look at the tire treads."

She shooed him away with her free hand. "Then do it. I want my horse back unharmed."

Hunter approached. "Rache is right. With Sam and the men coming in to work this morning, the yard is pretty messed up. I'll bet they planned on that."

Vince watched the foreman mounting up by the house. "What time did Sam come in?"

"Six."

"Six." Rachel answered the same time as Hunter.

He liked that about her. She was sharp, knowing what would be important, like preserving the scene. It wasn't even light out yet at six, which meant the thieves purposefully came in the dark.

Hunter continued. "When you left it was after midnight. I didn't go to sleep until about four."

Rachel punched Hunter in the arm. "Why didn't you hear them?"

Vince had a feeling the only reason Hunter didn't turn her over his knee right then and there was because they were very old friends. Instead, he just looked at her.

She colored nicely at her faux pas. "Shit, I'm sorry. I just want my horse back."

Hunter nodded. "We got that. I didn't hear them because I was asleep. The same reason you didn't hear them."

Vince looked down the road. "That meant whoever took him rode him out of here to a waiting trailer between four and six this morning. A truck would have been heard." It also meant that the person who planned the theft knew Hunter was here and when he slept. Either that or they were just damn lucky.

She looked at the twine spread over the yard. "So Hunter didn't have to do that?" She pointed with her left hand, the right one holding the rifle across her body.

Vince started toward the area. "Actually, if my theory

is right, we should find horse tracks heading off the property and down the road. Your men may have rolled over some in their trucks, but my guess is they mount up by the barn and head out in the opposite direction from the driveway."

For the first time that morning, her fear for Foxglove abated. Vince made a lot of sense. She followed the men toward the corded off area and watched as they combed it for clues.

"Here." Vince stopped and pointed, then continued toward the driveway and out the fence, watching the ground. They walked a good half mile before he halted. "This is where they loaded him up."

She looked at the dirt. The tire tracks of her men were obvious, but there were light indentations here and there. He'd figured that out from those?

Hunter finally spoke. "Look at this tire track."

She and Vince moved to the side of the road where Hunter pointed at one of many.

"That's the same track that was in the west pasture." He looked at Vince.

"That's all I needed to know." He took a few photos then smiled smugly.

She looked at both men. "You know who took Foxglove?"

He nodded. "I do. The man's a thug. He's working for someone else. It's time for me to pay him a visit."

Hunter put his hand on Vince's shoulder. "You want back-up?"

"No, not yet." He came over to her. "I'll be back this afternoon. Any chance you have any of those monster cookies left?"

Cookies? The man was worried about cookies? "You bring me back Foxglove and I'll bake you two dozen cookies."

He tipped his hat to her. "That's all the incentive I need."

She winked at him. "That's all?"

Despite Hunter standing right there, he pulled her against him as his mouth came down on hers.

This wasn't a gentle kiss either. It was a hot, passionate, triumphant kiss that had her feeling lightheaded when he pulled away. Vince had definitely changed over the years. She liked it.

He nodded once to Hunter and strode toward his truck.

"You going to keep him this time?" Hunter's voice startled her.

As usual, she was totally engrossed in Vince. She turned to look at her old friend and smiled. "Yeah, I think I just might."

He didn't say anything, just turned then walked with her back to the ranch.

She was happy with the silence, her mind too preoccupied with how to make the evening a rewarding one for herself and Vince…assuming he found her horse.

Chapter Seven

Vince parked around the corner of the apartment building in an older section of Austin. It wasn't seedy like where he'd expect to find the usual lowlife, but it was definitely less traveled.

Visions of children picking through the garbage in the alley way behind restaurants threatened to take him off track. This was for Rachel. He had to refocus.

The buyer of the bull had been more than happy to take his money back in exchange for the bull when he discovered the Sheriff at his door. Vince liked to stay friendly with law enforcement because there'd been many times they'd done him a favor.

He locked his truck and walked behind the building. Now, he just needed to find Foxglove and return him as well. Looking around, he found exactly what he'd come for. He smirked. It wasn't hard to determine which truck had had a bull in the back.

He walked to the white pick-up and looked inside

the bed. Good work, Matterhorn. The inside was completely busted up and the tailgate was held on with rope. A large tow hitch stuck out from below the bumper for pulling trailers. Pretty much every pick-up worth its salt in Texas had one.

He crouched down next to the driver side rear tire and scratched at the dirt in the tire's tread. Interesting how even after a half-hour drive, there could still be rocks and dirt in there. He pulled his phone from his pocket and scrolled to the picture he'd taken of the cast Hunter had made.

It was a perfect match, even down to the wear on the outside. This man really should have his truck aligned more often. Vince took a picture of the tire then slipped his phone back into his pocket. This was the truck that hauled off the bull and Foxglove.

He leaned against the bed of the truck and folded his arms. Now to wait. He didn't mind. He was a patient man.

His gut tightened as he remembered Rachel's face when he first jumped out of his truck. She loved that horse, and he'd be damned if he didn't get it back for her.

About twenty minutes into his wait, a young man drove in and parked near the door to the building. He looked back at Vince and nodded then hurried inside.

Shouldn't be too long now.

Seven minutes later, the apartment building door opened and a middle aged man in jeans and a gray checked shirt stepped out. His hair was limp and past his ears. He had stubble on his chin and a mustache.

"Hey, cowboy. What 'er you doin' leaning against my truck?"

"Waiting for you."

The man strode closer and squinted up at him. Near sighted? "Why?"

"I'm looking to buy a Quarter horse. A blue roan that could produce some smart looking foals."

The man spat. "I don't know who told you I could help you, but I'm not in the horse selling business."

Vince could smell alcohol on the man's breath. This early in the day was a good sign he dealt with a drunk and a drunk could be easy to intimidate… sometimes. He moved a step closer to the man, emphasizing his height. "That's not what I hear. Let's talk price."

The man shook his head. "I tell you, I don't have no horse to sell." He spread his arms wide. "Does this look like stables to you?"

He took the final step that put him within arms-length and grabbed the man by his shirt. "I'm not playing around. I want that horse. Now tell me who I talk to to get it."

The older man's eyes had widened, but then they turned shifty. "Sure, I'll put you in touch with her."

"You work for a woman?" Hell, it was the last thing he wanted to hear.

He shrugged. "It keeps the boss happy, so I do it. Besides, it pays well." The man motioned with his head toward the building, indicating the nice digs he scored with his better pay.

Vince loosened his hold on him. "So where can I find the woman who'll sell me the horse?"

"I'll call her. Set up a meeting."

"You do that." Vince let the man go so he could make the call on his cell.

When the man was done, he hung up. "She said to meet her at the Seventh Street Cafe near Springer Street at noon."

"Good and if this is a set up, I'm coming back here and breaking both your legs."

The man shook his head. "No set-up. Just be sure she knows Jack gets the referral fee."

"Right. I'll do that, but one thing before I go. Who's this boss you're trying to keep happy?"

Jack's smile disappeared fast and he looked around, his gaze darting across the area. "He's just the boss. No name. Now, I gotta go."

Old Jack was scared shitless. Good. That meant if Vince had to come back here, it wouldn't take long to get the info he wanted. "You go. I got a date with a horse."

Jack moved away, mumbling beneath his breath about pushy cowboys. Vince let him go. He didn't plan to get involved with the filth in the city again. He'd asked out of habit. Now he had to find out who the woman was.

He already knew, but this would be the final evidence he needed. He walked back to his truck and started it up. The cafe wasn't too far from where he was and he had an hour, which meant it was a good opportunity to scout places nearby that might hide a horse.

By eleven thirty he gave up on finding the horse and waited across the street from the Seventh Street Cafe, his truck parked two blocks away. He didn't need it to be recognized.

He wandered around the shop he was in, pretending to look at the knick-knacks and craft supplies, while keeping his eye on the cafe. Having spent all the time he could there, he walked out and into the alcove of the doorway next door. He pulled his phone out and pretended to be on a call.

When noon hit, relief settled in since he didn't recognize any of the women who entered the coffee shop across the street. He was about to put his phone away when a taxi pulled up to the cafe and let out a passenger. She stepped out in an aqua blue dress and matching purse and heels. She rushed into the place as if she were late.

Vince lowered his phone. *Crystal.*

Not taking any chances, he stepped into the store he'd been standing near and pretended to look at the bronze statues by the window. Crystal came out and looked down the street and then up and finally across. He stayed behind the angry bear near the door so she wouldn't spot him.

Finally, she got on her phone and made a call. She stepped to the curb and hailed another cab, still on the phone. The fact she hadn't come out of the cafe with a cup of coffee or a scone or something, made it clear she'd been expecting to meet the buyer of Foxglove.

This would kill Rachel. She would hate him forever if he did this. "Fuck."

"Excuse me, sir?" A young woman with attitude looked down her nose at him.

She probably heard him swear. He faked irritation. "I just banged my knee on this statute. That's the last thing I need in my house." He limped to the door as Crystal and her taxi drove away.

Once outside, he took a deep breath, but the smell of car fumes and grease filled the air. He didn't miss his old job at all. Now, he had to make sure he had an air-tight case before he presented his findings to Rachel.

Unless he could return the horse and the money with her none the wiser.

There was a slim chance he could keep this between himself and Crystal. To do that, he needed to be able to confront her with everything.

Determinedly, he wove between the people on the street, anxious to return to the ranch where there was clean air and Rachel.

~~~~~

Rachel finished setting the table. The fresh cut wild flowers toppled from the vase in pretty purples and yellows. The steaks would be ready in just a few minutes, but the door to her office remained closed.

Vince had insisted on working privately all afternoon. Normally, she wouldn't have agreed to that, but since he'd found Matterhorn, who arrived a couple hours ago, and had even called her insurance company so she wouldn't be accused of insurance fraud, she let him do what he did best.

She now had complete faith that he'd find Foxglove but she hadn't made the cookies yet. She'd promised them for when he found her horse and he still searched. She crossed her arms over her waist. She hoped her boy was okay.

The sound of the office door opening and Vince's boots on the hardwood floors had her surveying the kitchen table one last time. Then she watched the doorway, her heart beating just a bit faster.

He stepped in, his face worried, but the minute he looked at her, he smiled. He walked straight to her and took her face in his hands. "You don't know how good it makes me feel to see you."

Before she could respond that it had only been a few hours, his lips were brushing hers and nudging her to open her mouth. She held his waist and let him in. His tongue dove in, tasting her, mating with hers, making her knees weak.

When he let go, her hips fell back against the counter and she grabbed it to steady herself.

"That closed door did little to block the heavenly smells coming from this kitchen." He took a deep breath. "I hope dinner is almost ready."

She nodded as she regained her equilibrium. "It is. Could you grab us a couple beers?"

He moved to the refrigerator.

She didn't miss the opportunity to look at his ass in his blue jeans. The man was even hotter now than when they first dated. Forcing herself to look away, she piled the steak, mashed potatoes, and peas onto two plates and set them at the table. She grabbed the gravy she'd made and brought it as she sat down.

Vince raised his beer. "To a bright future for the Sunnyview Ranch."

And to us. She grinned and clinked her beer bottle against his then drank. When she put her bottle down, he was already cutting into his meat. "Does that mean you've figured out where my money went?"

He nodded, his mouth full of steak.

Relief swept through her and her stomach loosened. Maybe she could actually eat her dinner now. If he knew where it went, then she had faith he could get it back.

After a few moments of companionable silence, Vince looked at her instead of at his food. "This is excellent. Thank you for inviting me to dinner. I rarely get a home cooked meal."

She stopped, her fork on the way to her mouth. "Why? Because of your job? Are you gone a lot?"

He sat back, titling his head to the side. "Actually, no, that's not why. It's because it sucks cooking for one person."

Oh, she probably shouldn't have jumped to negative conclusions. "I get that. I cook with the anticipation that Crystal may drop in, so when she doesn't I have great leftovers."

"Does she ever?" He sat straight again, as if her answer were important.

"Yes, she does. Usually two or three times a week. With her, she has such a busy schedule, especially before tax time, that she is lucky if she can get to the vending machine for dinner. The other times of the year, she is having fun with her friends, so she goes out to eat a lot. She likes coming here for home cooked meals." She put another forkful of mash potatoes in her mouth as he visibly relaxed.

"You two seem closer now than when she was young."

She swallowed. "We are. We're all we have left of our family besides the ranch."

Vince's brow lowered in concern. "No aunts or cousins and all that?"

She shook her head. "No. My mom was an only child and my dad was the youngest of two but his older brother died young as well—heart attack."

Vince appeared to chew on that along with his steak, so she took another bite of hers. That he was concerned at how little family she had left was comforting. Of course, if she and Crystal were to have children, then they could have more family. She would love to have a bunch of kids running around the ranch, playing in the hay, learning to ride, helping a baby calf come into the world.

"What are you thinking about?"

She'd stopped eating with her thoughts, and Vince looked at her curiously. What would their children look like if they married? "I was just daydreaming. Will I be able to get that lost money back? Was it a hacker like I thought? Or was it a huge mistake on Crystal's part? I don't think I could tell her if it was. She is very proud of her ability to manage the finances here."

He finished eating. "I don't think you'll get your money back. It *was* a big mistake on Crystal's part, but it's something we can correct moving forward."

"Oh." She didn't know what to say to that. She'd rather it had been someone stealing her money than for Crystal to have made such a huge error. Now she would have to double check all her work. When would she have time for that?

Vince rose and lifted the dirty plates.

"Oh no, I can do that." She rose as well, already reaching for them.

He pulled them away. "No, you cooked the meal, so I should clean up."

Really? That was almost too good to be true. "Okay."

She picked up her beer and leaned against the wall so she could watch him. Hunter had asked her if she would keep Vince this time around. She definitely wanted to. She was in a better place now than before. It wouldn't have worked out for either of them when they were younger.

The question was, did he forgive her? Sometimes it seemed that he had, but other times, she wasn't so sure. Like yesterday when they'd had sex. He hadn't even taken his boots off for criminy sake, yet he seemed to enjoy it. She kept getting hot and cold vibes from him.

She took a sip of beer and enjoyed her view. Vince had a tan shirt on that stretched over his powerful back as he scrubbed the pots to put them in the dishwasher. Even without his hat or clothes, anyone would know he was a cowboy through and through. How did he ever fool all those criminals?

"Done." He shook out the dishtowel and folded it over the towel holder. "Now for dessert."

She pushed away from the wall as she rapidly thought of what she could give him. She moved to the cupboards and opened the one she kept snacks in. "I didn't make any cookies because Foxglove isn't home yet." Now she felt like a louse for being so literal. She should have made them to show him she had faith that he would bring her horse back because she did.

His arms wrapped around her from behind and he spoke in her ear. "That wasn't the dessert I had in mind."

A shiver of anticipation ran through just before his lips touched her neck beneath her ear and she giggled. She scrunched her shoulder up. "I'm ticklish there."

He turned her around in his arms. "I know that, but it makes you giggle and you don't do enough of that." His face turned serious. "You need to take time for yourself."

She opened her mouth to protest, but he placed his finger across her lips.

"Hear me out. There is more to life than running the ranch, taking care of Crystal and helping your hands. You're still young, twenty-nine if I remember right. You need to live." His gaze softened. "You need to love."

Lord have mercy, she did. "I want to, but if I don't do all that then everything will fall apart. I'll lose it all."

He shook his head. "Not if you let me in. Let me into your life, Rae. Let me help you. Let's actually live life together.'"

Her palms started to sweat and her eyes itched. "I

want to, I do. I'm just not good at depending on someone other than myself."

He gave her half a smile. "Are you depending on me to find your horse and fix your money problem?"

She looked away from his mesmerizing gaze. Was she? Shit, she *was*. She looked back at him. "I *am*." She couldn't keep the wonder from her voice, surprised she'd been able to let him help her.

He brushed the stray strands of hair back that always fell around her face, his touch gentle, like she remembered. His eyes finally returned to her gaze. "Let me in."

Her view started to blur. "You're already in."

"Ah Rae, it's not so bad, is it?"

She shook her head then nodded.

He chuckled. "I can help you get used to it."

She blinked away her tears, not happy with them at all. "But what if you disappear again? I can't do that. It ripped my heart open last time. I was so worried you were hurt or dead and I didn't know. No one would tell me."

He pulled her into his embrace and held her tight. "I'm sorry. I was so caught up in my own misery, I didn't think what it had to be like for you." He pushed her back so he could look at her. "I promise, I will always stay in touch with you, no matter what my job requires of me or I won't do it."

She widened her eyes. "Really?"

"Really. I love you, Rachel. I've never stopped loving you."

She closed her eyes as joy barreled through her then

opened them again and smiled. "I love you, too. I always have."

He threw up one arm and shouted. "Yes!"

She laughed, letting her happiness fill her completely. Then Vince's mouth was on hers, sweet yet passionate, like the man he had become. Wrapping her arms around his neck, she kissed him back with all the love she felt, tangling her tongue with his and pressing herself against him.

He broke their kiss and leaned his forehead against hers. "I never thought this day would come. You've softened all the sharp edges in my soul."

She rubbed her fingers along the base of his hairline. "I didn't know how empty I was until you filled me."

He pulled his head back. "I want to fill you again. I want to feel myself glide into you with nothing between us."

She liked that idea. Liked it a lot, but she didn't know where he'd been or who he'd been with since they parted. She'd been tested long ago and it wasn't as if she'd slept with anyone since then. Plus she was on birth control, but she still had to know. "Are you safe?"

He pulled away and she thought she'd angered him again, but he grasped her by her hips and sat her on the counter.

"I wouldn't have suggested it if I wasn't."

"I know. But I had to ask. That independent thing again."

He ran his hands down her bare arms. "Never apologize for who you are. I love that you're independent."

He moved his hands under her white shirt and lifted it up and over her head. "This time, it's about you."

She grinned. "I was with you last time, too."

"I was selfish and not very considerate." He leaned toward her to wrap his arms around her and unhook her bra.

She took his face in her hands. "You needed something from me. I got that. Sometimes one person needs more than the other. We can give and we can take. If we love each other, we don't keep a tally. Okay?"

He brushed her lips with his own. "You are one of a kind, Rachel Henderson."

She smirked. "I know."

He laughed then pulled her bra from her arms. "And I'm going to show you exactly how special you are." He gazed at her breasts as if he'd never seen them before.

This time she wanted to see the older him, too. She grasped him by the shirt and pulled him toward her, opening her legs wide so he could come closer. "I'm looking forward to it." She unbuttoned his shirt down to where it tucked into his jeans and yanked it up. "But I need this shirt off you to really appreciate the experience." She finished unbuttoning the last buttons and the ones on his sleeves before pushing it over his shoulders.

Vince shrugged out of his shirt, caught it with one hand and threw it on the table. "Anything you want."

Chapter Eight

Rachel gazed at the muscles outlined on Vince's chest, his taut nipples making her own harden. His abdominals were rippled with a nice crease down the center. But it was the enticing start to the V called the Adonis Belt that disappeared under his jeans that had her sheath moistening. With that strength, she knew how hard he could thrust into her. She wiggled her brows. "Be careful what you say."

He brought his fingers to her waistband and unbuckled her belt, flicking the leather end. "Hmm, I think as long as you aren't into ropes and whips, I'll be okay with it."

She scrunched up her nose. "That's not my style. I don't even use whips on my horses."

He leaned forward, placing his hands on the counter on either side of her, his lips only an inch from her hardened nipple. "That isn't a surprise." His breath caressed her peak and her areola reacted, wrinkling up.

She arched toward his mouth and her nipple brushed his closed lips. His tongue shot out and licked her. The sensation zinged from there straight down to her opening. She grasped his head. "More."

This time, he spoke against her breast, his lips moving seductively over her. "As I said, whatever you want." He licked around her hard nub then gently sucked it into his warm mouth.

Her sheath tightened. "Yes."

Vince's suction on her breast grew slowly until it verged on pain, yet she grasped his head tighter against her, her whole body tingling with desire now.

He loosened his mouth around her and brought his teeth to close over her nipple.

She held her breath, expecting a nibble or a bite.

He closed his jaw just slightly than wiggled it back and forth, effective rolling her nipple. She held onto his head to keep herself upright as her whole body turned to mush.

Take me now. The thought vibrated through her body, but she was greedy. She wanted more.

And he gave her more. He let go of her nipple and kissed it gently then kissed a trail down her breast to lick a path up between them both before continuing to her other one. She expected him to perform a similar treatment there and she held her breath in anticipation.

Vince wrapped his arms around her and pulled her close as he sucked as much of her breast into his mouth as possible while his tongue laved at her nipple. That action alone had her melting, but when he let out a groan of need against her skin, it vibrated down to her core and into her heart.

"Take me, Vince."

She wasn't sure he'd heard her as the suction on her breast continued and his tongue played some more, causing the ache inside her to become almost unbearable with unfulfilled desire.

He finally released her, only to bite at her nipple with short, sharp nips that had her crying out her pleasure. Finally, he stood straight and wrapping a hand behind her head, kissed her deeply.

She pressed her bare chest against his, feeling her breasts give way to the hardness of his pectorals. The differences in their bodies made her feel hotter and very female.

When he finished taking over her mouth, he lifted his head. "Where did you want me to take you?"

It took her a second to register what he said, but as a crooked smile formed on his face, she remembered her own words and laughed. "Take me wherever you want, just take me."

His smile was smug as if he'd known exactly how to make her pant with need, but she didn't care. She was ready.

"As I said, whatever you wish." He moved one arm under her legs and the other behind her back. "Hold on."

She grabbed him around the neck as he carried her out of the kitchen. "Vince, I'm too heavy."

He brought her into the living room, to the couch she'd fallen asleep on just the night before. He laid her down and stood staring at her in the glow of the single lamp. "No, I think you're just right."

She had no waist and her legs were too long, but if he thought she was perfect, who the hell was she to argue? "I think I need to see more of you before I decide if you're just right."

He raised a brow at her statement, but his hands went to his belt buckle. She watched as he unbuttoned and unzipped his jeans then toed off his boots. Without hesitation, he dropped his jeans and stepped out of them, his thigh muscles bulging as he picked up the pants and threw them on the coffee table.

Then he pulled down his white underwear and stepped out of it, throwing it to land on his jeans. His cock was hard and sticking straight out, as if it were looking for her. She certainly hoped so.

The play of muscle in his torso and legs as he lifted one leg then the other to strip his socks from his feet had her almost salivating.

He held his hands out to the side. "So?"

She gave him the biggest smile she had. "I like." She winked. "Perfect."

He knelt next to her to unbutton and unzip her jeans, but not before she caught a slight flush in his cheeks. Had she embarrassed him with her compliment? That she may have, had her heart sighing. He truly was perfect.

He pulled off her boots and socks then gave a tug at her jeans.

She lifted her hips and he slid them off then turned around and placed her pants on the rocking chair. Her smile froze on her face at two large scars on his lower back and a wisp of memory from the last time they made love came to her. "Were you shot?"

His hand came to his lower left side as he spun around. "Yeah. Just a case of taking action before my back-up arrived."

The reality that she might have never seen him again sunk in deep—all because she'd pushed him away. "You must have had a good reason."

He scowled at the memory, his whole naked body tense. "I did. They were going to rape a thirteen year-old girl. I couldn't wait."

Her belly did a somersault. "And you stopped it?"

He nodded though his hands had fisted at his sides. "But she got hit with bullets, too."

She swallowed hard, afraid to ask her next question, but needing to know. "Did she live."

He nodded, but didn't say another word, the tic in his cheek reappearing.

She could see his mind sifting through his horrible memories. He would stew on them, but she wouldn't let that happen now. She was here this time.

They needed a change in topic. She wiggled her hips. "I think I have too many clothes on."

His eyes refocused on her and the tension left his cheek. "Let me see if I can do something about that." He knelt again and hooked his thumbs in her practical pink cotton panties.

She lifted her hips, and he slid them down her legs, but not before she saw the wet spot on them.

He pulled them off and threw them on the rocking chair to join her jeans. Then he looked at her and his warm brown eyes darkened. "You're ready for me."

She flushed that he'd seen the evidence, but played it off. "I am."

He remained kneeling. "What would you like next?"

"I'd like you to make love to me."

His nostrils flared. "Good because that was my plan." He ran his hands up the outside of her bare legs to her hips then stroked them down the inside of her thighs, pushing her leg on the outside of the couch aside until her foot touched the floor.

Her heartbeat kicked up a notch as her folds were clearly in view now.

"I want to taste you, Rae."

Oh Lord, she hoped he didn't expect an answer because her throat closed up so hard at his statement that she couldn't even swallow. Their private time together years ago had been minimal and oral sex had not been the priority. She knew what his mouth could do to her breasts. What could he do to her below? Just the idea had her juices seeping again.

Vince leaned forward as he brought his hands up the inside of her legs straight to the juncture of her thighs. His gaze was intensely focused on her there as his fingers spread her labia, revealing her opening to him.

Every nerve ending became sensitized as her blood rushed to where his fingers played.

He brushed her natural blonde curls upward, lightly grazing her clit as he did so.

She barely kept herself from jumping.

"Beautiful." His words, whispered on an exhalation of breath, permeated her brain, making her flush.

She had no time to be embarrassed. His head descended and she felt the first swipe of his tongue as he licked at her opening.

"Hmm." His vocalization vibrated against her, causing her sheath to contract.

He licked again, holding her nether lips open so he could taste her fully. He pressed himself closer to the couch like a man starved for sustenance as his tongue burrowed into her opening.

Instinctively, her hips pushed upwards, but his elbows held her down, forcing her to lay back and enjoy. She tightened around his tongue and he groaned again. Her entire body shivered with need, ready for penetration.

Then he pulled his tongue out and licked up and over her clit.

"Oh wow." Her exclamation was torn from her as her entire body jerked at the touch.

Once there, he didn't leave, his tongue playing with her sensitive nub, rubbing it upwards and side to side, every movement sending her closer to orgasm. Desperately, she tried to hold on, to wait for his entrance.

Vince let go of her labia and pushed two fingers into her sheath.

Her hips came up of their own accord, despite his weight on one side. The feeling intensified as he started to pump in and out with his fingers while his tongue continually played with her clit.

When he lapped upward against her clit double time, she lost it. Her sheath tightened around his fingers, grasping hard as her clit vibrated with pleasure. She gripped the couch and pushed her pelvis against his tongue, prolonging the exquisite ecstasy.

He slowed his tongue on her sensitive nub as he pulled his fingers away.

"Oh Lord, that was—"

She didn't finish. Vince lifted himself over her and kissed her with her own taste on his tongue. She'd never done that before and the eroticism of the experience had her body revving up again.

He lifted his mouth from hers and she opened her eyes, no clue when she'd closed them. His dark gaze was filled with promise and need. She pulled his face to hers again and pushed her tongue into his mouth.

His moan was her only warning before his bare cock entered her to the hilt.

At his penetration, her body lit up like a firework and she squeezed him tight, loving the feel of him inside her.

Vince didn't move a muscle, even when she pulled her lips from his. "Are you all right?"

His eyes opened. "Better than that."

She grinned. "Me too. This is right."

He nodded, but still didn't move. So she squeezed him again and his eyes widened. "I'm going to come."

She practically purred. "That's the idea."

"Now."

That simple word combined with the look in his eyes set off a chain reaction inside her, so when he pulled back and thrust into her hard, she splintered.

Vince rocked her body as he pumped into her, sending her orgasm soaring into the atmosphere. His groan of pleasure grew louder until he shouted, spilling his semen into her and jumping with her to another level of satisfaction.

They lay there catching their breath. Vince somehow kept himself from crushing her. She didn't have an iota of strength left in her and she didn't care. She was happy, purely happy for the first time since she'd sent him from her life.

The stars had finally aligned for them. It was their time.

"I'm guessing from your scream that I did as you required?" He'd lifted his head and looked at her with one eyebrow raised in question but a prideful smile on his face.

She smiled back at him. "Perfectly."

He lowered his lips to hers and gave her a gentle kiss that reminded her of the kisses he used to give when they were younger.

She loved the mature Vince even more for having the old one inside him.

The sound of a car pulling into the yard sent her thoughts scattering. "Shit. Someone's here."

He looked over his shoulder. "It's Crystal."

His tone made her pause for a moment before panic set in. "We have to get dressed."

"It would serve her right for dropping in unannounced."

She hit him on the arm. "Don't be silly. This is her house, too."

He gave her an odd look, but she was too busy pushing him away so she could get up and dress.

He sighed and slowly separated them.

The loss of him inside her made her want to call him back, but that just wasn't possible. She looked outside just as her sister exited her car. "Uh-oh."

Grabbing up her jeans and panties, she ran into the kitchen and started dressing. She'd just hooked her bra when she heard her sister's high-heeled tread on the porch steps. Pulling her shirt over her head, she looked for her socks and boots. "Ah, shit."

Vince pulled on his underwear, jeans, socks and boots then waited. He didn't plan to hide what he and Rachel had done. Crystal needed to know that there would be a lot of changes now that he was here, the first being that she needed to confess.

Crystal entered the house. "Rache, I just heard. I'm so sorry." She closed the door then stepped into the living room and stopped. "Oh, hi Vince." Her gaze swept his naked torso. "I take it you were comforting my sister over Foxglove and things went too far?"

He didn't smile. "No, they went exactly as they were meant to go. Why would I be comforting Rachel about Foxglove?"

She sauntered into the room, her navy blue suit with

matching heels and purse made her look every inch the executive. The expensive floral perfume she wore was not to his liking at all. "Didn't she tell you? Foxglove is missing."

He watched her like he'd watch any perp. No eye contact, exaggerated voice inflexion. Hell, even if he didn't have all the damning evidence, which he did, he'd suspect her. "How did you hear?"

She looked at him startled. "Where's my poor sister?"

"I'm right here." Rachel strode into the room and gave Crystal a warm hug. "You heard about Foxglove?"

Crystal nodded. "I'm so sorry." She put her arm around Rachel and steered her toward the kitchen. "Have you called the Sheriff? What did he say?"

Vince followed the women into the room and nonchalantly picked up his shirt from the chair he'd thrown it on and shrugged into it.

Rachel sat in the chair across from him while Crystal pulled two glasses from the cabinet. Rachel looked at him, and he shook his head, knowing she would tell Crystal the truth.

He wanted to give Crystal a chance to come clean. "I spoke with the Sheriff and it appears they have a good lead on who took the horse." Crystal paused for a split second, not enough for Rachel to notice, but he did. He was quite sure Rachel was as surprised by his announcement as Crystal, since they hadn't called the Sheriff.

Crystal finished pouring two glasses of ice tea. "Oh, that's a relief. Who did it?"

He moved to the cupboard and pulled out another glass and placed it next to the still empty one. She looked at him in surprise, but smiled graciously.

"The Sheriff said it was some guy named Jack who works for a known loan shark, but this time he was working for a woman."

Crystal didn't pause this time. She spilled the tea, missing the glass completely. "Oh sugar. What a mess."

Rachel rose to help her, but Vince motioned her back down. He plucked the kitchen towel from its ring and wiped the counter. "No harm done." He looked Crystal in her eye. "Mistakes happen. As long as we learn from them, then they are worth making."

Crystal's eyes widened with understanding.

"From spilling tea. I don't think there's much to learn from that." Rachel's voice cut through Crystal's surprise.

"Here, maybe you better pour." Crystal handed him the pitcher. "I've had a stressful day." She turned away from him and took the chair at the head of the table.

He didn't pour. He left everything as it was. "Why was it stressful? Couldn't you find a buyer for Foxglove?"

"What?" Rachel frowned at him. "Why would…no."

Her voice trailed off, the hurt almost more than Vince could bear, but he needed Crystal to tell her.

Crystal looked at him as if he had spouted horns. "What are you talking about? I would never sell Foxglove. Besides he's not even here." She looked at her sister. "I'm sure the Sheriff will find him."

Rachel moved her gaze from her sister to him. She begged him with her eyes to tell her what she thought he said wasn't true, but as much as he wanted to, he couldn't give her that.

He'd thought long and hard about confronting Crystal privately and never telling Rachel, but he didn't want to live with that wedge between them. It would come out eventually and she would never trust him again.

He shook his head at her and returned his attention to Crystal. "You didn't get nearly half Matterhorn's value. If you weren't in such a hurry, you could have raked in more. Then you wouldn't have had to take Foxglove."

Fear showed in Crystal's eyes, but he steeled himself against it. "Luckily, I had that paltry sum and was able to reimburse Matterhorn's buyer. He's out in the north pasture even as we speak."

Crystal turned to Rachel. "Rache, I don't know what he's talking about."

"I'm talking about the condo you own on the twenty-seventh floor of Sky Towers, the thousand dollar bar bills at Seventh Heaven, the six hundred dollar pair of heels you're wearing and the five hundred square-foot closet that houses your designer suits and dresses."

"Crystal?" Rachel's face showed so much pain, he couldn't go on.

Chapter Nine

Maybe it had been a mistake to confront Crystal with Rachel in the room. Vince still hoped Crystal would confess.

"Rache, these aren't the real thing." Crystal lifted her shoe for inspection. "You know I like the nice stuff, but I buy the fakes. I can't afford anything else. You know that."

Rachel closed her eyes.

His heart went out to her. He should be protecting her from this, but Crystal had a problem and Rachel had to see it.

Crystal turned and glared at him. He didn't blame her, but he also felt no guilt. Maybe if she confessed, neither would she.

Rachel opened her eyes and stood. She looked at Crystal. "Get out." Her voice had no emotion to it at all. "Just get out." He knew Rachel was hurting, and he wanted to help her through it.

"What? Rache, this is my home." The whine in Crystal's voice grated on his nerves.

The woman he loved suddenly changed, her voice turning to steel. "Apparently, it isn't. You have your own home. Get out of mine."

"But I'm your sister. All you have left."

Vince walked over to Crystal and pulled her up to stand. "Let's go."

She glared at him. "Where are you taking me? Let go of me."

He moved her toward the door of the kitchen.

"Rachel, don't do this. I didn't do anything. It's not me. It's him." She glared at him then a smirk curved her face as they walked down the hall. "It's him, Rache. Vince is trying to come between us. He resents my bond with you. He wants the ranch for—"

He opened the front door and brought her out into the night. She stopped yelling as he walked her down the steps. When they arrived at her car, she struggled to be free and he let her go.

She turned on him like an angry bull. "How dare you do that in front of my sister?"

"I dared because I have all the evidence. I know the CR Seed and Grain Company is just a funnel for you to receive money. CR, Crystal Rachel, not hard to figure out. And Dr. Fielding's bills as well. As if soaking the ranch for your penthouse wasn't enough, you needed to make your sister think you were getting help so you could buy your expensive clothes."

"I was getting help!" Crystal yelled loud enough that the horses in the barn nickered.

He kept his tone low. "Buying things isn't help. I investigated Dr. Fielding. There is no such doctor, only a clothing line with that name."

She turned away from him and opened her car door.

He grabbed her arm. "You need help."

She pulled her arm away. "I'm fine. You're the one who needs help if you believe what you're saying. My sister will hate you for this. You're the one who's screwed." She sat in her car and slammed the door.

He moved out of the way as she started the engine, not sure if she was threatened enough to commit vehicular homicide.

Crystal spun the convertible around and drove off the ranch, leaving a cloud of dust in her wake.

Vince watched the cloud settle to the ground, looking like snowfall in the moon's bright light. Finally, he strode back to the house, his heart hurting for the woman he loved.

He found her still in the kitchen, sitting in the chair she'd been in before, a blank look on her face. He moved toward her to pull her into his embrace.

She put her hands up. "Don't touch me."

His heart stilled. "Rae, I can help."

"Don't. Just don't. Leave me alone."

He knelt in front of her. "I can't. I won't. Not ever again."

She looked at him then, her pain so clear it was all he could do to not touch her.

"I wish you'd never revealed that. I want to be alone." She held up her hand as he opened his mouth to speak. "Just tonight. Please."

His gut told him that wasn't what she needed, but his heart said to give her whatever she wanted. "Okay. I'll be back tomorrow morning, if you're sure that's what you want."

Her eyes grew shiny with unshed tears. "I am."

Hell, how was he supposed to walk away from this woman when she was in so much pain? It was like leaving a friend bleeding to death while chasing down the man who shot him.

He couldn't do it. But he'd let her think he would. He rose. "I don't think this is a good idea." Her head snapped up, her face angry again. "But I'll go."

The relief in her eyes was not what he wanted to see. Was she anxious to be alone or to do something drastic? "I'll be back tomorrow."

She nodded, already looking through him with that blank stare that made his gut twist. With more willpower than he thought he had, he walked away and left the house. As he strode toward his truck, he created a plan.

Getting in, he started it and drove down the road. When he was out of the view of the house, thanks to a small patch of trees, he parked it on the side and started his walk back.

This time, he would stay right where he belonged.

~~~~~

A loud banging on the front door forced Rachel to

open her eyes. The sunlight streamed into the kitchen, making her close them again. They felt puffy and sore.

More banging had her covering her ears.

Shit, all right already. She thought about moving then promptly put her head back on the table. Blessedly, the banging stopped.

Voices in the house had her opening one eye. The low tones meant men. Her men were in the house? The sound of cowboy boots heading upstairs jogged a memory of Vince and her making love.

She closed her eye. That was something she'd like to dream about.

"Rachel!"

Now what? Couldn't a girl sleep on her kitchen table in peace if she wanted to? She opened her one eye again. Why was she in the kitchen?

The scene from last night barreled through her head and she jerked herself upright. Her sister had stolen from her. Her sister. Crystal.

"She's down here."

She jumped at the sound of Hunter's voice behind her. "Shit, could you not do that?"

The man ignored her and moved to the sink. As he filled the coffee pot, the sound of footsteps grew louder until Vince was there, standing in front of her. He crouched down and brushed the hair out of her face. "Hey."

She looked into his eyes and saw a shitload of sympathy. It brought her tears back, her mind flooding with the memory of sitting here bawling her eyes out. She shouldn't have any water left in her to cry.

She sat back away from him. She'd be damned if she would cry any more over being a fool. "Morning."

His brow knit with puzzlement. "You okay?"

She took a deep breath, dispelling her need to cry as she latched onto her anger. "Yes, I'm all right. I'm no longer the fool I've been."

Vince shook his head. "It took Hunter and me days of work to figure this all out. There was no way you could have known."

She shook her head. "The signs were there, I just didn't see them."

Hunter put a hot cup of coffee in front of her. She gave him a grateful look and picked it up. "I don't understand why she did it. She loves this place." She took a sip, both loving and hating the liquid for waking her up more.

"She does love this place. That's why she always returned enough money to keep the ranch solvent. If you hadn't received that notice, you wouldn't have known, though your bull and horse would still have been taken."

She pushed the other cup of coffee Hunter had placed on the table toward Vince. "Explain please."

He ignored the coffee but sat in the chair next to her, taking her hand in the process. "Crystal had your two most valuable animals taken so she could sell them in time to replace the money she owed your checking account."

"But why did she need so much money?"

Hunter sat down across from them. "She lost her job last month. The firm got tired of her coming into work late after her nights out on the town."

She looked back to Vince. "But why is she spending so much? It's not like we were poor growing up, and the ranch could handle our needs even after our parents passed. The only time money was tight was after Mom died and the medical bills came in, but we made it through okay."

Vince squeezed her hand. "It's not about the stuff. I'm no psychiatrist, but my guess is that Crystal buys things to compensate for the loss of your parents, maybe even her baby."

A strange relief flooded her at Vince's suggestion. His explanation of Crystal's motivation made her actions possible to accept. It didn't excuse them, but it fit better with the sister she knew and loved.

"Damn, you sound like one of my old therapists." Hunter quirked a smile.

Vince shrugged. "That's the theory I like best. The other is that she purposefully wants to bring the ranch to bankruptcy."

Rachel sucked in her breath at the hurt that rifled through her heart from his statement. She didn't like that one at all. "I'm going with your first theory, which means we need to find Crystal some help."

Vince took a sip of coffee and looked at Hunter.

"What?" She didn't like the sinking feeling in her stomach at that exchange.

Vince squeezed her hand again, a sure sign she wasn't going to like what he said.

"She's committed a number of crimes and she needs to be held accountable for those crimes. The state can provide her with the therapy she needs."

"The state? You mean prison? Oh no, I am not sending my sister to prison. I can get her the help she needs right here. I can bring her back to the ranch. Keep an eye on her."

Vince shook his head, but the sound of a truck pulling into the yard had all three of them looking out the window. He turned to her with a grin on his face. "I think this is something that will make you feel better."

She looked out the window again and noticed a trailer attached to what looked like Vince's truck. The driver stepped out and moved to the back of the trailer. She glanced at Vince who was grinning ear to ear.

Foxglove?

Without asking the question, she rose and headed out of the room. By time she opened the front door, the driver was tying her beloved horse to the corral rail. Joy burst in her heart and she ran to her stubborn stallion with open arms.

He neighed a welcome and she hugged him around the neck. "Thank the Lord you're safe." Tears fell to her cheeks as she rubbed her face against him, but she didn't care. Her boy was back.

Then she smoothed her hands over him, checking for any misuse or damage, even cueing him to lift his feet so she could inspect his shoes. When she was done and satisfied he was none the worse for wear, she kept a hand on his side and watched as Vince paid the driver.

Both her boys were back. Maybe she needed to make her man a more permanent fixture at the ranch.

Vince strode toward her, his look so confident she couldn't resist. She ran to him and jumped into his arms.

He caught her as she knew he would. "I love you, Vince Gallagher. Will you marry me?"

His wide-eyed look of shock sent her into laughter before she could speak. "Of course, you can think about it if you want."

Hunter walked over to them. "What do you say, buddy?"

Vince looked into her eyes. "I say yes."

She whooped before giving him a kiss worth her weight in love. When she was done ravishing his mouth, she gave him her best coy look, which she'd bet was pretty pathetic since she'd never looked coy in her life. "Um, I forgot a ring."

Vince's laughter filled her heart. "That's okay. We can go shop for rings together."

She gave him another kiss then he set her down, his arm securely around her shoulders, keeping her by his side. She liked that.

"Now we just need to find Crystal."

At Hunter's pronouncement, she sobered. "What do you mean find her?"

"She didn't go back to her condo last night. The man I have watching it said no one has been there since she left yesterday morning."

She could feel the tension in Vince's body. "She may be on the run. She knows I have evidence against her and probably hopped the first plane she could get out of Austin. I'll call Roscoe and see if he can get a man to investigate flight passengers."

He looked at Hunter. "Do you have any buddies in surveillance? If she's driving, we might catch her using a credit card. I'll check her accounts and see if she withdrew any cash. Or she may have her phone on and we can track her GPS location."

Vince looked at her. "If you know her friends, it's a long shot, but it couldn't hurt to call and see if she flopped at their house for the night."

She frowned. "How about if I call her and ask her to come home?"

Both men looked at her and smiled. Vince shrugged. "It can't hurt to try."

"My phone is in the house. Let's try the easy way first."

~~~~~

Forty-eight hours later, Vince sat in the diner, waiting for Hunter. He sure as hell hoped he'd heard something. Rachel tried to hide it, but he knew her and she was worried.

They could have met at the ranch, but if it was bad news, he didn't want Rachel to know immediately. As long as Crystal's body didn't show up at the morgue, there was hope. His biggest fear was that Crystal was now in physical danger. Since he'd stolen Foxglove from the barn Crystal housed him in, she couldn't pay the other half of what she owed the loan shark.

Hunter walked in and the conversation in the diner

quieted. There was nothing like a man in black whose boots didn't make a sound on the tile floor to bring a hush to a crowded breakfast place.

When his friend had slid into the seat opposite him in the booth and the same waitress gave him his coffee, black, Vince shared his fear. "The reason we can't find her may be that they have her."

Hunter shook his head. "I don't think so. She's good at hiding. I think she's still nearby because she wants to make amends with her sister, but not be sent to jail."

Vince took a sip of his coffee, the sweetened liquid a welcome addition to his stomach. "That's giving her a lot of credit."

"True, but I grew up with these women. They're smart. Despite Crystal's spending habits, she's no dummy." He paused to look at his phone. A happy grin spread across his face.

"I'm guessing that has nothing to do with Crystal?"

Hunter turned his phone over. "Sorry. Adriana is getting impatient with my absence."

"And that makes you happy?"

A sly smile split his lips. "She makes her impatience known by sending me naked pictures."

Vince whistled through his teeth. Hunter's late wife would never have done that, but by his reaction, he was happy Adriana did. Trauma really *did* change a person.

Hunter shook his head. "The question is, where would Crystal—" His phone rang.

Vince nodded. "Go ahead, take it."

His friend picked up the phone and read the screen. "Fuck, it's Crystal."

Vince felt every muscle in his body tense. If anything happened to her, Rachel wouldn't be able to handle it. Not after throwing Crystal out.

"Crystal, where are you?" Hunter's low voice rose with his concern. "Okay, okay, slow down, he's right here." He held out the phone. "She says she has to talk to you."

A chill swept down his spine. Crystal wouldn't want to talk to him. Not after he revealed what she'd done. He took a deep breath as he grabbed the phone. "I'm here."

"Vince, they took her. You've got to get her back. They want the money. We need to give them the money."

He looked at Hunter. "Crystal, slow down. Where are you?"

Her panic came through loud and clear. Maybe she would slip up and he'd figure out where she was.

"It doesn't matter. They took Rachel."

His blood froze as his heart skipped a beat. "Who took Rachel?" How the hell did someone get to her? She was out with her ranch hands today.

"It's the guy I owe money to. He says I was late on my payment and I have to pay double if I want her back. Vince, he said if I didn't pay by midnight he was going to sell her!"

"Calm down. We're going to get her back. But you have to work with me." Vince looked at Hunter who scowled.

"I never meant for this to happen. I just couldn't

stop buying things and the banks wouldn't give me a loan because I already had too much debt." Crystal's voice was squeaking with hysteria. "Leo told me not to worry as long as he gets his payment. You have to help me. Rachel's all I have left."

Vince stifled his own panic, but his stomach was eating itself from the inside out. "Crystal, listen to me. I will help you. We can do this. I need you to go to Rachel's bank and withdraw all the money you need."

"I can do that." She sounded surprised by his request. "What if there's not enough?"

Fuck. How much did she owe? "Take the balance out of savings if you need it. Then I want you to arrange to meet him to bring him the money in exchange for Rachel."

"Okay. So what are you going to do?"

"I'm going to save you both. When you have the money, and the time and place for the exchange, you bring it to the ranch and I will take care of it from there. You got that?"

Crystal's breathing calmed. "Yes. I withdraw the money and call Leo and set a time and place then bring the money to the ranch so you can handle it. I'm guessing I don't let him know you will be dropping it off, right?"

"Exactly. It's time to outsmart this bastard."

"I like that idea." Crystal's voice lightened a bit. "See you at the ranch." She ended the call.

He handed the phone back to Hunter, letting his insides settle to a dull ache. "You better tell Adriana I'm going to need you a little longer."

His friend's look was deadly. "They took Rachel."

"Yes. And we're going to get her back."

Chapter Ten

Rachel couldn't see a blasted thing. The black shirt wrapped around her eyes fell past her face, making it hard to breathe. She lowered her head, which let air in under the shirt.

Vince, I could really use your help about now. He did say he would help her, always. Her heart ached for him. She didn't need this added touch of danger to understand how much she needed him. Shit.

Her hands were tied behind her back with rope, not the most comfortable position when sitting against a wall on hard concrete.

It was just her luck that she'd stayed behind to fix a cut wire in the fence while her men moved the cattle to the south pasture. Then again, that wire may have been purposefully cut. She'd been a sitting duck for the goons who'd taken her. She already knew one was Jack, the man Vince had mentioned to Crystal, but she had no idea who the second one was.

They had thrown her in the back of a pick-up truck and put a tarp over her. Her body had a dozen bruises from bumping along in the truck bed all the way to what she was certain was Austin.

The two men had handed her over to two other men who said they would hold her for the boss. This wasn't a good situation. They were probably going to ransom her or like Vince had told her, sell her or even rape her or both. She shivered involuntarily. This definitely wasn't Crystal's doing. Her sister would never put her life in jeopardy.

Maybe Vince or Hunter had come too close to figuring out where Crystal was, so the "boss" kidnapped Rachel as a distraction. She liked that theory the best. Whatever reason she was here, she had to figure a way out.

She continued to work at the rope that held her hands behind her. Her shaking fingers didn't help, nor did not knowing if she had a guard watching her. She didn't dare make big movements.

She always carried a utility knife in her back pocket when working the ranch and the guys who trussed her up never even checked. Once they found her phone, they stopped checking her pockets. Were they clueless about what a cowboy did for work?

Her wrists were raw from the rope, but she was making progress.

She listened carefully to every sound. The heat of the day caused the building around her to make cracking noises. It had to be a metal roof of some kind, so maybe a warehouse. She didn't mind those sounds. It was human footsteps that made her nervous.

The rope snapped and she stilled. No one said anything. With one hand, she folded her knife up and slipped it back in her pocket. Then she rolled to her side, holding the rope around her wrist with one hand while she brought her free hand up against the wall to lift the shirt away from her eyes just a little.

No one was there. She looked all around her, but there was no one. She was just left against the metal wall behind a row of boxes that looked like appliances. Did they smuggle ovens across the border or something?

She took a deep breath, trying to calm her shaking body. Freeing her other hand quickly, she stood, her cowboy boot scraping against the concrete. She froze at the noise, and listened. It sounded like no one was in the warehouse, but her two guards must be here somewhere. Picking up the rope, she tied it around her waist. Maybe they would forget where they'd left her.

Opening her mouth to speak, she promptly shut it. Not a smart move. Talking to herself could get her killed right about now. As quietly as possible, she slipped her feet from her boots and held them in her sweaty hands. She had to find a way out without running into one of her guards.

She felt like she was in one of those video games her sister used to make her play when the character couldn't tell what was around the next corner but the player could. Ah, now that gave her an idea.

Looking up at the boxes of ovens stacked higher

than the roof of her house, she didn't relish the idea of falling off and having them land on her. She moved her gaze higher to the ceiling where the metal braces held the roof up. A walkway for changing the light bulbs ran down the middle of the warehouse. If she could get up there somehow, she could figure out how to get out.

Stepping up to a stack of ovens, she checked to see if she could peek between the stacks. But they were tight. She kept moving down the line. One spot halfway down had a slight crack that let her see there was another row of appliances next to the one she was in front of.

When she reached the end of the row she listened, her fear escalating. She could barely make out voices. She tried to catch words, but couldn't. Finally, she screwed up her courage to peek around the corner.

The warehouse was huge with at least twenty rows of stacked appliances. At the other end was an office with a window. Two men watched television in there. Shit, who had time to do that in the middle of the day? She backed up so they couldn't see her and moved closer to the outside wall she'd been leaning against so she could study the one perpendicular to it.

The wall to the office was just metal with a support every ten feet or so, but no door. She really hoped the door to the place wasn't by the office, though she was well aware that it probably was.

At least knowing where her two guards were, calmed her shaking a bit. She headed back down the aisle she'd come and carefully peeked around the corner at the other end.

Halfway down were two large metal doors where the semi-trucks must bring in the merchandise. There was no small door that she could see, but there was a ladder that went all the way up to the ceiling.

She slowly padded her way toward it, checking each row before crossing in case there were more men scattered throughout the warehouse. She made it to the ladder with no incident, but now she had to figure out how to climb it while holding on to her boots.

Seeing no way to do it, and not wanting to leave her boots there, which would clue in anyone who walked as to her whereabouts, she put them back on and started to climb.

She didn't mind being up in the second level of her horse barn or even on the top of her hay bales when she threw them down, but the warehouse was taller than that and her hands started to sweat. Just what she needed, to fall to her death because she was afraid she'd fall to her death. "Not smart, Rachel." Her voice though a whisper, had her stopping.

She waited, watching the floor below, her hands sweating even more. When there was no new movement, she wiped one hand on her dirty jeans and grabbed the next wrung. After doing that with her other hand, she focused on what was above her, not below.

When she made it up on to the catwalk, she sat and let her heartbeat return to normal. From here she could see one half of the building. There was a door, but as she suspected, it was next to the office.

She'd just have to crawl to the other end and see if

there was any other way out. She rose on her hands and knees and started to make her way across, keeping her boots away from the metal to avoid making any noise.

She was almost halfway across when she heard the small door to the warehouse open. She froze.

Vince studied the warehouse specs on his phone for the twentieth time. There were only two ways in, a single door on one side and two loading bay doors on another. Most likely they would have Rachel away from the small door to make sure they had their money before letting her go.

He didn't think they'd let her go unless they had kept her blindfolded. Only then would she have a chance. His best guess was their plan was to take the money, take Crystal, take Rachel and leave.

He glanced at Hunter, who crouched next to him behind the dumpster they used for cover. The man was tense. Like himself, Hunter probably had memories of similar situations and his reflexes were on overdrive.

In that building, somewhere in the eight thousand square-foot space was his woman…and she needed him.

Vince looked at his watch. It was time to get into position. He nodded to Hunter, who acknowledged the signal and slipped away. At least he had a well experienced man to help him extract his future wife. He'd thought briefly of bringing in the police, but was afraid they would scare Leo the loan shark away before he could get to her.

His plan with Hunter was simple. Whoever found

Rachel first, brought her out of there. They each wore an ear piece and the only words they would communicate were "got her" and "blowing the doors" if needed. The other person would engage the perps if necessary and they would all exit. The meeting place was a nearby bar.

It was time. He walked back into the alley and strode around the block to the side of the building where Leo was expecting Crystal. A black sedan with blackened windows drove up just before he turned the corner. That had to be the boss man.

He ducked behind the corner of the building and watched as three men exited the car and walked into the building. Two had semi-automatics, the third didn't carry a weapon in sight, but he was sure to have one.

After they went in, he continued his walk toward the warehouse, the backpack of money all that Rachel had left. He didn't care. She was worth every penny and more. Nestled in the money was a small explosive device that would do little except send men to the ground and expel a bunch of smoke.

The grenades were in his jacket. If the criminals were smart, they'd figure the jacket was for weapons and take it, which was his plan. The other parts were well hidden in his hat.

He reached the door and knocked. One of the men with a semi-automatic opened the door. "Who are you?"

"Howdy." He played the hick cowboy pretty well. "Crystal sent me."

The man frowned, scanned the alley behind him then let him in.

Good. He gave the area a quick examination as he was escorted to a small office. Outside it, the other man patted him down. He pulled out the grenades. "What are these for?"

He shrugged. "Emergencies."

"Yeah, well there won't be any emergencies in here today. What's in the bag?"

Vince barely kept himself from calling the man an idiot. "What your boss is expecting."

The man frowned then his face lightened, but he didn't ask to inspect the bag. Not smart.

"Where's Crystal?"

Vince shrugged. "Hiding. She was too scared to come, but wanted her sister back, so she sent me. I'm getting paid to drop this off and bring her sister home."

The guy shook his head. "The boss ain't going to be happy about this." He opened the door and pushed him inside. "You can tell him yourself."

~~~~~

Men's voices floated up to her. Rachel lifted her head above the short railing and saw three men enter.

"This can't be good." She covered her mouth with her hand as her pulse went into overdrive. She listened intently, but all she could hear was the pounding of her heart. She had no idea where the men were in the warehouse, but at least she didn't hear anyone climbing the wall ladder.

She had to get out—now. But how? She looked down the rest of the cat walk to the other end which hung out over open space. She looked back but she knew what was there and there was no way out that way. Below her were just stacks and stacks of appliances. Unless there was some kind of trap door in the concrete floor, that wouldn't help her. Lastly, she looked above.

Lord have mercy! Not much farther than where she knelt was a hatch in the ceiling. She looked back toward where the men had come in. She could just see the head on one man talking to someone else.

She really didn't have a choice. Crawling to the spot where the hatch was, she examined it. There was a latch, but no lock or anything. The question was, how much noise would the rusty latch make, and while she stood to undo it, she'd be in the line of sight of the men below.

A knock on the outside door drew her attention and she watched the men she could see move toward the door. Okay, it was now or never. Standing up, she worked the rusted latch, hoping the voices below would drown out her little noise.

Not wanting to know if they saw her or not, she screwed up her courage and opened the hatch. It seemed like the sun that streamed in was a spotlight centered on her. Ignoring the fear in her throat, she hoisted herself up through the opening and quickly closed the hatch quietly.

She sat listening for a moment before the heat of the metal roof began to burn through her clothing. "Shit."

Taking her boots off again, she pulled her socks

from her feet then shoved her feet back into her boots, which turned out to be no small feat. Putting her socks on her hands, she knelt and looked over the entire roof.

For criminy sake, she felt like she was on top of a skyscraper! "Stay calm and do what Vince would do." She studied all four edges of the building. Behind her, it looked like something metal rose above the roof line.

Since there was nothing else but mechanical pieces, she crawled toward the object. As she drew closer, she started to relax. It looked like the top of a ladder. Quickly, she finished her quiet trek, feeling more confident that her kidnappers didn't know she was up there and that she would be able to get down.

As she reached the edge, she looked over. "Yes." Between the two loading bay doors was a ladder. She pulled her socks from her hands and stuffed them in her pocket. As she swung her leg over onto the first wrung, she thought seriously of tying herself with the rope she still had around her waist as a safety precaution, like mountain climbers did, because it was a long way down, but she didn't want to take the time to untie herself. Besides, the rope wasn't very long.

She took a deep breath and studied the area in front of the bays and into the alleyways. No one was about. Gripping the side of the heated ladder with her hands, she swung her other leg over and started her climb down.

It seemed like forever and she was too nervous to look down, so she focused on the metal wall in front of her and not on how high she was or how hot the ladder was on her hands. It wasn't until she tried to place her foot on the next rung and found nothing there, that she finally looked down.

The ladder ended a full story above the ground. Shit! What good was a ladder that didn't go to the ground? Who the hell designed this piece of work? Her anger helped her conquer her fear as she stood there, a sitting duck for anyone to see, her hands beginning to burn.

Okay Vince, now would be a great time to find me. But as she scanned the immediate area again, there was no one around. She looped her arm over the rung and held on by the crook of her elbow to give her hands a break. *Come on, Rachel. You can do this. You run the ranch. You can certainly get yourself down off a ladder.*

Her options were limited. She could jump and possibly break her leg, but she could crawl for help. Or she could stay on the ladder and hope the Calvary came, but the fact was, she didn't know if anyone even realized she was missing. If she waited, there was a better chance the kidnapper would find her. If she took off her shirt, she could possibly hang three feet closer to the ground and—"You're an idiot. You have a rope."

She looked around to see if anyone heard her, but the place remained empty.

Suddenly, gunfire erupted inside the warehouse.

Shit! Quickly, she untied the rope from her waist and secured it to the bottom rung of the ladder. Thanking her dad for teaching her rope tying, she let herself dangle then grabbed the rope and lowered herself. At the end of the rope, she looked down.

Triumph rumbled through her and she let go, dropping the three feet to the ground. "Now to ge—"

A hand over her mouth stifled her words and her success.

Chapter Eleven

Vince tipped his hat to the man sitting in the old cloth office chair with wheels. That must be Leo. The man sported a goatee, long side burns and was skinnier than a fence post. He was probably about twenty-five, so a newcomer in the business. Maybe picked off an older boss to get where he was. Vince had seen his type a dozen times before. "Howdy."

Leo scowled. "Where's Crystal? Who are you?"

"Crystal sent me. Where's her sister?"

He pulled the backpack from his shoulder and plopped it on the desk next to Leo, pretending he didn't see the other two men in the room. He unzipped the backpack showing the money so they would think he played by their rules.

"Whoa."

"Fuck."

The two men's reactions behind him told him what

he'd thought. This little crime boss had never received such a huge sum.

"I brought you the money. Now I need the woman."

Leo motioned with his head and one of the men in the office left. Good, now there was only two he needed to take out.

"I hope Crystal's sister is okay. I hear she's dating some ex-police officer." He purposefully didn't mention Rachel's name. If they didn't know it, he didn't want them to, and just thinking her name twisted up his insides again.

Leo tensed, but didn't say a word.

"Shit boss. That's all we need." The guy behind him wasn't as savvy as his boss.

Leo waved his hand like it was no problem before wiping the newly formed sweat from his forehead.

The other man who'd left ran in. "She's gone."

Leo stood. "What do you mean, she's gone?"

"Like disappeared. No ropes, no girl, nothing."

Fuck, where are you Rachel? He hadn't counted on that variable. Fear for her started to eat at his confidence.

Leo scowled, but his look turned crafty. He shrugged. "I guess you're too late." He sneered. "Maybe she went shopping."

He pretended he didn't care and started to zip up the bag. "Then I'll bring this back to Crystal and be on my way."

Two guns against his back had him freezing.

Leo grinned. "I'm thinking you leave that right here and go on your merry way. What do you say, cowboy?"

He looked over his shoulder as if he'd never been held at gun point and raised his hands. He needed to give Hunter time to find Rachel. "I don't want no trouble, but I don't get paid if I can't bring back the money or the woman."

"Then I guess you don't get paid."

He pretended to be concerned. "Heck, I need to make my rent."

Leo laughed and pushed his finger into his chest. "Then you best find yourself another job, cowboy."

It was exactly what he wanted, all of them close to him. He nodded. "Okay, okay." He tipped his hat, detonating the explosion in the bag.

All three hit the floor. He grabbed the guns from the two on the ground and stepped aside as one of the men with the automatic weapon stepped into the room. "What's going on in here?"

He shot the man in the gut then used him as a shield to get out of the office. The other semi-automatic went off, riddling the man with bullets. Vince shoved him forward and dove behind a forklift.

"I've got her." Hunter's words coming into his earpiece sent a wave of relief through him, releasing his anger. *Finally, this cowboy's break.* Crouching low, he aimed beneath the forklift and shot.

The semi-automatic man fell. Vince rose and aimed again, shooting the man in the chest, ending his misery.

"Blowing doors now." Hunter's voice sounded in his ear and Vince ducked back behind the machine just as the main doors blew.

Leo ran out of the office and Vince made an instant decision. He stepped out from behind the forklift and shot Leo in the head.

Bullets came out of the office door and he dove for cover once again.

"I've got her." Hunter's voice in her ear had her sagging in relief.

She let him pull her away from the warehouse to a spot behind a nearby dumpster. He let go of her mouth and grabbed on to her wrist like a handcuff. He didn't say anything, just stood there watching the warehouse.

Too shaken to think, she waited with him. Finally, her brain started functioning again. "Where's Vince?"

He nodded toward the warehouse.

"What? No, we have to go help him."

He finally looked at her. "No, *we* don't."

"But—"

"If we go in there, we'll pull his attention away from the men he needs to focus on. Just wait." Hunter returned his gaze to the warehouse.

She tried to swallow her fear because Hunter did make sense, but it wasn't her brain that needed convincing. It was her heart.

Hunter lowered his head "Blowing doors now." He pressed something on his belt and the large bay doors burst apart. Metal went flying everywhere and he pulled her down as it hit the dumpster.

Shit.

Twice she heard gun shots and twice she tried to run

back, but Hunter wouldn't let go. She hated him right now.

"What if Vince is bleeding to death?" She couldn't help voicing her worry.

"Let Vince do what he does."

Sirens in the distance gave her some relief. At least they would go in and save him. Hunter started to pull her away. "What are you doing? You can't leave him in there."

"It's all part of the plan."

"What plan?" She kept looking over her shoulder trying to see the warehouse.

"It's important that the police not discover the part you played in all this. If they find Vince there, he will be questioned and released pending further investigation. We're to wait in the bar around the corner for an hour. If he doesn't come by then, it means he went with the police."

"Or that he's dead." She practically screamed the last word, her hysteria rising.

Hunter turned her toward him and grasped both her shoulders. "Don't lose it now, Rachel. We're almost home free. You have to have faith in Vince's abilities."

She swallowed down her panic. "I'll try."

"Good girl. Now let's go order some food and I think you could use a beer."

They walked in and chose a table within sight of the door, but farther back. After ordering, she took a swig of beer. "This isn't helping."

"I didn't expect it would."

"Then why—"

Hunter sighed. "Because you needed a distraction. Have a little faith."

She nodded and took a gulp in hopes it would give her the nerve she needed to get through the next hour.

The sirens converged behind the block. As the police drove by, some of the bar patrons watched then went back to their conversations.

"So how did you get on the roof?"

She kept her gaze on the door to the bar. "I climbed one of those ladders that go up the side wall. It went to a bridge of sorts. I wanted to find an exit and looked over the whole space from up there. The only door was by the office, so I thought I was stuck."

"But you weren't."

She shook her head, her mind still hearing the gun shots inside the building. "No. There were the big loading dock doors, but if I opened one of those, they would catch me before the door rose high enough for me to get out."

"Or shoot you."

She looked at him and shivered. "Right. I didn't think of that or I might not have stayed calm enough to get out." She turned her head back so she could watch the door. "Since I couldn't go down and get out, I looked up. There was an access to the roof. Once I got out there, I crawled to that ladder down the outside."

She turned back to face Hunter. "You didn't have to grab me like that."

He raised a brow. "I didn't want you to scream."

She took another sip of her beer. "I wouldn't have—okay, maybe I would have."

Hunter's chuckle aggravated her, which wasn't fair, but she was just too anxious to see Vince. What if he was killed?

"But you didn't tell me how you got loose. You said the rope you hung from was what they tied you up with."

She reached into her back pocket and pulled out her utility knife, her complete focus on the entrance to the bar.

Hunter's laugh, caught her off guard.

She looked at him. How could he be so sure Vince would be all right? Her stomach tightened even more, rejecting the beer she'd had. She swallowed hard to keep it down. When the fried mozzarella sticks and barbequed wings came, she thought she would vomit.

"Excuse me." She rose then ran to the bathroom. Despite her roiling stomach, she didn't get sick. After cooling her face with cold wet paper towels, she made herself leave the room.

When she stepped out, the first thing she saw was Vince, sitting at the table with Hunter. Her heart leapt and she ran to him.

He saw her coming and rose to squeeze her tight against his chest. They stood like that for minutes. She didn't care what others thought. All she cared about was that he was safe and whole.

He finally released her only to take her face in his hands and kiss her gently.

"Hey, you two. Get a room." The customer who called out laughed.

She didn't. "I love you with all my heart."

"I love you too, Rae. Your heart will always be safe with me."

She laid her head on his chest, reassured by the sound of his heart beating. She tilted her head back. "Can we go home now?"

He glanced over at Hunter who waved them off.

"Yes. Let's go *home*."

Epilogue

Rachel flipped the pancakes over on her griddle while Crystal set the table. Vince was on the phone with Aron McCoy, giving him a nudge about his hereford order, and her two guests were still upstairs.

She doubted she'd see Hunter and Adriana until noontime. Those two were up all night getting reacquainted.

She flipped the pancakes onto the stack and placed the plate into the warming oven. Now for some scrambled eggs. While she whipped up her eggs, she grinned. She liked Adriana once she'd talked to her.

When Adriana had shown up yesterday evening in her tight jean shorts, half shirt tied beneath her large breasts, black cowboy boots that matched her shiny black hair, and an old straw cowboy hat on her head exuding steamy sex appeal, Rachel had been taken aback.

Luckily, Adriana hadn't noticed. Her eyes had been

only for Hunter. Once introductions were made, they all settled in for a chat and a chance to debrief as Vince said.

Crystal was under "house arrest" as far as Vince and Hunter were concerned. Rachel just wasn't sure what to do about her now.

Vince came in and wrapped his arms around her waist from behind and kissed her cheek. "All done. They want delivery next week."

She sighed. "Thank you. That withdrawal for my ransom really hurt."

"I know, that's why I transferred a hundred thousand dollars into your checking account so you could continue operations."

She spun around. "Vince Gallagher, you did not."

"I did. This is soon to be my home too, so I want it to be functioning properly. That is, if you still want me as your husband."

She wasn't sure what she thought about the money issue, but he did have a point. It would take some getting used to, having another person to help her.

He turned her back around. "Don't forget your eggs."

"Oh shit." She scrambled them up quickly, adding seasoning and pieces of bacon. When she was done, she put them in a casserole dish to keep warm in the oven while she made toast.

The sound of cowboy boots coming down the stairs distracted her. It couldn't be Hunter. Adriana stepped into the kitchen, Hunter right behind her.

"Hmm, something smells good. I think we may

have a cook who could give Selma a run for her money." Adriana addressed Hunter, but Rachel felt herself flush.

Hunter had told her how legendary the cook was at Poker Flat, so she knew a compliment when she heard it. "Everything's ready if you want to sit."

As chairs scraped back and talk ensued, it reminded her of the days when her own family sat around the kitchen table having a big Sunday breakfast. She loved the feel of the moment.

She glanced at Vince sitting next to her. He held the platter of pancakes so she could serve herself then she passed it on. The thought of having children resurfaced. She did want them with Vince. A couple boys and a couple girls would be nice. The only problem was, she had to take care of Crystal.

Hunter put a forkful of pancake in his mouth and moaned.

Everyone stopped talking and stared at him.

He finished chewing then responded to the silence. "What? Can't a man enjoy his food? What did you put in these pancakes, Rache?"

Crystal spoke up. "It's a secret ingredient. We can't tell."

Rachel smiled. A little almond extract wasn't that big of a secret, but if Crystal wanted to claim it as a family recipe, she didn't mind.

"I think we should have a cook off between Rachel and Selma." Adriana spoke to Hunter but winked at Rachel.

Hunter shook his head. "Oh, no. We are not going

to upset the balance of the resort by bringing Selma competition. She's already refused to allow another cook in *her* kitchen."

"I have no problems with another bartender in my bar. I wouldn't be here if I did. Now we just need another receptionist, another stable hand, another—Wait. You said last night that Crystal has bankrupted this ranch with her spending, right?"

Hunter choked on his eggs. "I didn't say it exactly like that."

Rachel put her hand on Crystal's shoulder as her sister bowed her head in shame.

"Oh, no." Adriana waved off her comment. "I'm not saying it to be mean, but what if Crystal worked at Poker Flat?"

"At a nudist resort?" Rachel wasn't sure how she felt about that.

Hunter picked up on the idea. "The resort is all about second chances. You can't even work there if you haven't screwed up before."

Crystal raised her head. "I'd say this is more than a screw up."

"Doesn't matter the size." Adriana shook her head. "Do you have any skills?"

"She's great with numbers." Rachel beamed proudly at her sister.

Hunter, however, scowled. "That's the last thing she'd be allowed to do."

Adriana looked at Crystal. "Is there anything else you could do?"

Crystal shrugged. "Besides accounting, all I know is what I did on the ranch before I left home."

"Hell, that's perfect." Adriana smiled kindly. "Jorge needs help with the stable. You could even lead trail rides."

Rachel frowned. "They let nudists ride horses?"

"Yup. It's the only nudist resort in the country that figured out how to do it." Adriana beamed proudly. "I'll call Kendra if you want to try it."

Vince finally spoke. "Only if she can get counseling as well."

Rachel knew he thought Crystal should go to jail, but she couldn't stand the thought of her sister there. The only thing that had kept him from pushing that idea was the kidnapping and his role in killing five criminals.

Since he and Hunter had used weapons and ammo he'd picked up in Mexico when he'd waged war on the drug lord there, the police thought the warehouse shooting was no more than two criminal elements fighting each other.

But if Crystal was brought up on charges, everything might come out. She turned to her sister. "What do you think about working on a nudist resort?"

Crystal looked at her. "It wouldn't be my first choice, but I don't think I'm in a position to turn it down."

Adriana slapped the table. "Great. I'll call Kendra after breakfast. You do have to wear a uniform of sorts, basically dress like a cowgirl. But when you're not working you can go nude."

Rachel couldn't help herself. "Do you?"

Adriana nodded. "As often as possible." She hit Hunter with her elbow. "And with this man as much as possible." She winked.

Rachel smiled, happy that Hunter had a woman to fill his heart now. Maybe when Crystal was better, she'd find a man to love, too.

When everyone was finished with breakfast, they went about their chores and errands for the day. She stayed behind to clean up. Her sister wouldn't be dropping in anymore and that bothered her. It would be good for Crystal to get away from the ranch. There were too many memories for her here.

Rachel pushed the button to start the dishwasher then went in search of Vince. He was exactly where she expected him to be, in her home office, her dad's den. It definitely embraced Vince.

Wrapping her arms around him from over the top of his chair, she kissed his head. "Everything stable in here?"

He looked up at her. "Everything is accounted for."

She stood back and he turned the chair to face her. Before she knew what he was about, he pulled her onto his lap. "You seem a little sad."

"I am. I'm going to miss Crystal."

He brushed her hair away from her face. "I know, but it's not like she was here every day and now you'll have me here almost every day and definitely every night unless I'm on a work trip."

She sighed. "I know. It's just that having the kitchen full for Sunday breakfast reminded me of the happy times my family had in there. It feels right when there's so many people filling that big oak table."

He brought her lips to his and gave her a gentle kiss. "Then how about we work on building a family of our own?"

Her heartbeat went into double time. "Really?"

He chuckled. "Really. I love you Rachel soon-to-be Gallagher, and I would love to have a couple Rachels filling this house with joy."

"And a couple Vinces."

He raised his eyebrow. "Four children?"

She nodded, smiling.

"Then I guess we best get started." Vince kicked the door to the office closed with his boot, then proceeded to strip off her clothes.

She laughed with joy until his mouth found hers and their bodies became one.

For updates, sneak peeks, and special prizes, sign up to receive the latest news from Lexi at http://bit.ly/LexiUpdate

Read on for an excerpt from Wedding at Poker Flat (Poker Flat: Book 5)

Chapter One

Wednesday

Kendra Lowe absently reached for her ringing phone. "Yes." Her mind was on the profit and loss statement on her computer screen. Closing Poker Flat for five days for the wedding would hurt their bottom line.

"Sorry to bother you, boss, but I have a woman up here at the garage claiming to be your mother."

"What?" She glanced at the time. It was almost one in the morning.

"I didn't know I'd need a security clearance just to see my own daughter." Her mother's voice came through Mac's phone loud and clear. "Remind her she invited me to her wedding."

"Did you catch that?" Her security guard's tone held quite a bit of sarcasm, and she couldn't blame her.

"Yes, I did. Bring her down. I'll meet you."

"You've got it." Mac ended the call.

She looked at the small calendar on her desk. The wedding was still over a week away on Thursday. Her mother was supposed to arrive on Monday.

What the hell was she supposed to do with her mother with guests still at Poker Flat?

Quickly, she hit the keyboard and pulled up the reservations. "Well, damn." Scanning the list of rooms on the resort one more time, she closed it out and rose. Out of habit, she unclipped her dark hair and jammed the brown cowboy hat on her head. Grabbing up her sweatshirt, she strode out of her office toward the floor-to-ceiling glass double doors of the log and stucco main building.

Solar ground lights lit the desert pathways outside as well as the circular dirt area for golf carts when guests came in for meals or events. The area directly outside was empty, everyone in their casitas or at each other's depending upon their preferences.

Hopefully, none of them would go out for a midnight stroll and drop into the main building like one pair had last night. The last thing she needed was for her mother to stare in horror at a pair of naked guests.

She leaned on one leg and watched the dull yellow lights of a golf cart crest the other side of the ravine and slowly wind down the switchback path that led to a tiny stream bed. It would be a while before they crossed the bridge at the bottom and made it up to the main building.

She hated waking Wade up in the middle of the night, but there was no way around it. At least the new signal booster made it possible to have service now and she *could* call instead of having to drive over. It still didn't reach all of the resort, but enough. She pulled out her phone.

"What's wrong?" His deep voice on the other end settled her nerves far better than any drink could.

Just another reason why she loved him. "Sorry I had to wake you, but my mother just arrived."

"Now? Today?"

She could envision his warm brown eyes widening. "Those were my thoughts exactly, but it's really her. Mac's bringing her to the main building. She's going to have to sleep on our couch tonight."

The momentary silence was telling. "No casita available?"

It wasn't really a question. "No." She didn't want her mother in their space either. It wasn't that she didn't love the woman. She just didn't have a lot of respect for her. She had no backbone. Oh, she talked a good game, but when push came to shove, she always caved.

A heavy sigh sounded over the phone. "I guess there's no help for it. Don't get me wrong, I'm looking forward to meeting her."

She smirked. That was so Wade. "I know you are." He was the one who insisted she invite her mother. Actually, he'd asked her to invite both her parents but she drew the line at her mom. "Too bad we couldn't put her in the massage room, but I'm sure there are early morning appointments."

"And that wouldn't be very comfortable for her."

"What about Jorge's office? That has a nice big comfy couch in there. Far bigger than ours." The lights across the ravine had disappeared, which meant her mother was on her way up. "Do you know if any trail rides are scheduled tomorrow morning?"

"Hold on, let me check." The sound of her fiancé's

bare feet on the tile floor came through the phone before he pulled out the chair in their home office. "I thought the plane ticket you sent was for next week."

"It was." Which is why she was more than just a little confused. "I don't think it's even arrived yet." What was she going to do with her mother for a week? Poker Flat was a nudist resort and last she knew, her mother wasn't a nudist. Actually, she sincerely hoped that hadn't changed. That was a sight she really didn't want to—

"We're in luck. No rides tomorrow at all. Looks like the horses have the day off. I'll get dressed and run our extra set of sheets and a blanket over there. If you can grab a pillow from the linen room, she should be set for the night."

And that was another reason she loved him. He was one step ahead of her half the time. "I will. Thank you." She headed back down the hall to the laundry area.

"You know you'll owe me one."

She laughed, knowing exactly what he had in mind. "And I'll be happy to 'pay' up." She grabbed their last new pillow all wrapped in plastic and turned out the light. "I'm looking forward to it. The sooner the better." As she entered the lobby again, a glow of lights appeared near the ridge. "I have to go. She's here."

"Remember." Wade's voice held amusement.

Her heart warmed. "I know. You're all-in. See you soon, Cowboy." She ended the call and put her phone in the back pocket of her jeans before taking a deep breath.

As the golf cart pulled in front of the main doors, she strode forward, her cowboy boots loud in the empty building. Pushing one large glass door open, she smiled. Truth be told, she was excited to see her mother again. It had been a few years.

"There she is. The queen." Donna Lowe grabbed the side of the golf cart and unfolded herself from the seat with a grunt. "That was a long ass freakin' ride."

Ignoring the usual complaint, Kendra stepped forward. "Hi, mom."

Her mother, who was more than a few inches shorter than her, finally focused on her and gave her a brief hug, her rose perfume filling the air. When she stepped back, she squinted. "Did you get taller?"

"No, I'm the same height I was when I saw you last." Her mother's normally white hair was dyed a dark red now, but she had two inches of roots showing on either side of her part. She had it cut like a bob, but it was not well done and needed a good combing. Her eyebrows, which had been drawn on, were crooked and very large, making her look somewhat surprised.

The button-down shirt she wore to cover her own large chest was wrinkled and revealed more cleavage than a woman of her age should, but it was still a step up from her usual clothing. Her striped leggings made her skinny legs look even smaller. With her waist as big as her chest, people who didn't know her might think she would topple over like Humpty-Dumpty.

Her mother wiped her hands on her shirt as if they were sweaty. "I'm shrinking. That's what it is." She turned to Mac, who was seriously tall and fit. Not only that but with her black hair pulled back tight and in her black sweats, she was hard to see at night. "You're gonna bring my sweeties and the rest of my bags now, right?"

Mac shook her head. "Not until Kendra tells us where you're staying. Like I said, the resort is full." Mac moved her gaze to her. "Right, boss?"

She nodded. "We are, but I'm sure mom is tired, so we can put her in Jorge's office for tonight. In the morning, Lacey can work her magic I'm sure."

"Office? What? You expect me to sleep on a desk or something?" Her mother frowned, clearly expecting the worst. "Why can't I stay with you?"

"I'm afraid all I have is a small couch and Jorge's office has a big comfy one. Wade has already gone over there and made it up for you."

Her mother crossed her arms over her ample bosom. "The groom. I want to meet this man. I didn't inspect your last fiancé before that marriage and look how that worked out."

Her chest squeezed at the reminder of what an idiot she'd been. "Very true. I'm sure Wade will answer any questions you have tomorrow. I think we should get you settled in."

"To an office. Nice way to treat your mother."

Kendra ignored her mother's mumbled words. She had no doubt her mom would be thrilled with the accommodations once she saw them. "Mac, why didn't you just bring her bags down on the cart?" She'd noticed there was only one bag on the back.

Mac glanced at her mother. "Because we're going to need the wagon to get them all down here."

"What?" She looked at her mom. "What did you bring? The kitchen sink?"

Her mother's lips formed a slow, smug smile. "I would have if I could have cut the pipes."

Airlines charged per bag. Her mother didn't have that kind of money. In fact, she couldn't have received the airline ticket yet, since it had just been mailed two days ago. "Mom, how did you get here?" Even if she took the bus, a cab ride to Poker Flat would have been over a hundred dollars from the Phoenix station.

Her mother shrugged. "I drove."

She widened her eyes. "Drove? You and Fred bought a second car?" Could the man who produced her have pulled his act together after all these years?

Her mother laughed. "Not even close. I took the car, everything I could fit in it and all the money in our account. I've left your father. I'm going to live here while the divorce goes through. Aren't you happy?"

In complete shock, it took her a moment to notice the vibration in her back pocket. Turning away from her mother's triumphant smile, she answered the phone. "Yes?" Her voice came out in a whisper.

"Kendra, what's wrong?" Wade's voice on the other end had her heart clicking into a more normal rhythm. Only he had the sixth sense when it came to her emotions.

Taking a few steps away from her mom, she kept her voice low. "Mom just informed me she's divorcing Fred and plans to live here until she's a free woman."

Wade's low whistle on the other end reassured her he understood exactly how impossible the situation was.

"That's a big pile of shit to deal with at this early hour in the morning. Just bring her over here, and we'll hash it all out later."

"Right."

"That's awfully rude." Her mother's voice carried as it always did. "It's the middle of the fucking night and she has to take a phone call? I thought this was a nudie resort. Why do you have sweats on?"

Mac's low tones floated over. "Because staff are not allowed to go nude while working."

"That seems weird. You'd think everyone would be nude here."

Kendra took a deep breath. "We'll be right there." Ending the call, she spun around and strode toward her mom. "Okay, let's get you to bed."

"Who was that? Don't they know it's the middle of the night? I've been driving for hours just to see you and you take a call? What's wrong with this generation?"

She ignored her mom's complaining, something she'd learned to do at an early age. "Mac, I'll take it from here. You can grab another golf cart."

"Will do." Her crazy-fit female security guard wasted no time jumping into another golf cart and beating a hasty exit. Kendra didn't blame her.

Finally, she turned back to her mom. "If you'd like to climb back in, I'll take you over to the stable manager's office. It's a whole separate building and has everything you'll need including a full bathroom."

Her mother stepped up into the passenger side of the cart still grumbling. "Now you're putting me in a stable. What do I look like, Mary Magdalene? I'm not pregnant. I'm not fat either. Things just shifted. It's called post menopause and it will happen to you, too. Just wait. Hey, what about my stuff? Is that amazon going to bring it?"

She turned the cart on and pressed the pedal. "Not tonight. I want to get you a real room, so you can have your own space. There are no trail rides scheduled tomorrow, but I'm sure Jorge and Crystal will need to use the office at some point."

Her mother grabbed a hold of the side of the cart as they went over a rock. "So now I'm an inconvenience?"

"Of course not. We just weren't expecting you until next week. Every guest room is booked right now. It's winter and high season for tourists." She glanced at her mom. "I wanted to make as much money as possible so I can afford to feed all our wedding guests." That her mother would get.

"That's my girl. You take after me, you know. Your father couldn't keep a nickel in his pocket if it was stuck in there with chewed gum. But me—" Her mother's smile became devious. "I know how to stretch a penny and save. What your father doesn't know won't hurt him."

Her stomach lurched. She didn't want to know, but her gut told her she would soon be learning all the sordid details. She was torn about her mother's announcement. Half of her was damn proud of her. Fred had always treated her mother like crap. She'd even stopped calling him dad at the age of nine because she couldn't stand the thought that they were related in any way.

But the other half of her worried about the repercussions of her mother's decision, both in what might happen for her mom and how it would affect herself and Wade. Fred wouldn't take his housekeeper and cook skipping out on him laying down.

She drove the golf cart up the slight incline toward the barn and office. Despite knowing she'd probably regret it, she had to ask. "Why did you finally leave Fred? He didn't hurt you, did he?" The thought of him hitting her mother had her hands squeezing the steering wheel.

"Of course not! If he dared lay a hand on me, I'd beat his flabby ass from here to kingdom come."

She relaxed. Fred was an unfaithful asshole and a drunk, but he'd never done anything physically abusive. He didn't have to, his mouth did it all for him.

"Then why did you leave him now?"

Her mother grinned. "When you called and said you owned a resort and were getting married, I figured you had finally settled down."

Okay, that might be true, but what did that have to do with leaving Fred? "I don't understand."

"It's simple. Sally left the park after her husband died and moved in with her son and daughter-in-law. Betty's daughter renovated her garage into a mother-in-law apartment so Betty could leave that falling apart trailer she was living in. And now I can move here to be with my daughter."

Kendra was back to squeezing the steering wheel as she pulled to a stop in front of the stable manager's office next to the golf cart already parked there, her shock and fear so complete she wasn't sure she could move.

Luckily, Wade opened the door and strode out. Her broad-shouldered, thin-waisted cowboy had a smile on his face as he walked toward her mother's side of the golf cart. "You must be Donna. I'd know you were Kendra's mother even in a crowded fair. You're obviously where she got her good looks."

Her mother looked at her and rolled her eyes before turning back to Wade. "Well now, if that ain't a crock of shit I don't know what is." She waved him toward her. "And you just keep piling it on, honey."

Wade chuckled as he tipped his hat, barely revealing his short chocolate-brown hair beneath. "I'll do my best, ma'am."

Her mother looked over at her again. "Is he for real?"

She managed a weak nod.

"Well, damn me to hell and back. I'm gonna like it here." Her mother turned toward Wade, who offered her his hand to help her out. "Oh, yes, I'm going to like it here a lot."

As Wade guided her mother into the office, she forced her fingers to let go of the steering wheel. Already her mind was racing with one disastrous scenario after the other. Her mother insulting a guest. Her mother getting drunk at the bar. Her mother spinning out on a golf cart and it toppling over. Her mother walking into her house when she and Wade were having sex. Her mother stalking into the kitchen to complain to Selma about her meal.

She lowered her head onto the steering wheel and closed her eyes. Maybe if she wished hard enough, she'd discover this was all just a bad dream.

"Hey." She looked up to find Mac standing next to the golf cart.

She scanned the area but didn't see another cart nearby. The woman was as quiet as Hunter, her other security guard, and both of them did a fantastic job. Would they be willing to escort her mother off the property? She shook her head. That wasn't an option. Nothing was an option, and that scared the hell out of her.

"Anything I can do?"

She shook her head. "No. Not yet anyway. She just informed me she plans to live here. Indefinitely."

Even in the low illumination of the single spotlight on the outside of the barn, Mac's shiver was clear. "That will be…interesting."

"Hah." The understatement was laughable. "Far worse than that." She pulled herself together and exited the cart. "Did you need something?"

Mac's mouth formed a grin. "Yes, I was wondering what you wanted me to do with the dogs."

"What dogs?" She scanned the dirt area in front of the barn, but didn't see any dogs. She didn't even hear a coyote, which was odd.

"Her dogs." Mac pointed toward the office. "They're in her car. I didn't realize they were there because they were so quiet, but I was just up there and they must have woken up because they are yapping like crazy."

Dogs? Her mother didn't have any dogs. Last she knew her mother didn't like dogs. For that matter neither did she. They were too much like coyotes for her comfort. As if her childhood trauma had happened yesterday, her left leg started to itch. She really didn't like dogs. "Are they big?"

Mac shook her head. "I've owned cats bigger than these dogs."

Her tension eased. That was the first good news she'd had all night, which in itself was pretty sad. "You better bring them down here. Put them in the unfinished Saloon."

"I'll check and bring anything in the vehicle that might help. She was adamant about locking her car, but then she handed me the key to bring down her bags."

Kendra waved the idiosyncrasy off. "That's typical. I'll have Wade and Jorge get the rest of her things once I find out from Lacey where and when we can move her."

"Got it. I'll be back."

Mac strode off, disappearing into the desert beyond the circle of light. She knew far more about Mac than anyone on the resort and she was proud at how the woman had fit in. She'd kept more than her fair share of vandals off the property. That and the teenagers with more curiosity than brains.

Squaring her shoulders, she moved toward the office. If she left Wade alone in there with her mother any longer, he might think twice about marrying her. Even at the thought, her gut twisted. Here she was the one who had delayed the wedding plans and now she wished they'd eloped before he ever met her family.

Luckily, there was just the one. Fred was not family.

~~~~~

Wade barely kept himself from laughing out loud as they exited the office and he guided Kendra to his golf cart. Her mother both shocked and amused him, mainly because she was the complete opposite of her daughter.

Kendra sat in the passenger seat and opened her mouth to speak.

He put a finger over her lips and shook his head.

After she nodded in understanding, he walked around to the driver seat and sat next to her. Turning the cart on, he drove toward to their house, the only two-story adobe place on the resort. Once they had passed the Old West town, the newest addition to the resort, he glanced at her. "Go ahead. Spill."

She frowned, which was far better than how she used to register her frustration, which had been showing no emotion at all. Still, he knew the frown was just the tip of the iceberg with his soon-to-be wife.

"She wants to live here. Did you hear that? On a nudist resort. The wedding isn't for another week and she's already moving in. And what the hell are we going to do with her until then? I can just see her making fun of a man's penis and the next thing you know, we'll be all over the nudist internet as the place to avoid. I didn't build this place just so she could kill it."

Kendra took a breath, so he jumped in. "I'm sure

she doesn't want to ruin your livelihood. You're her daughter."

"You don't understand." She shook her head. "I'm not saying she will purposefully ruin me. You heard her in there? She doesn't have a clue what she's saying."

He chuckled. "You mean about how she understands now why you went for such a big piece of meat?"

Kendra groaned. "Everyone except you would be pissed off by that. I can just imagine what she'll say when she—Oh, hell."

"What?" Even in the dark, he could see the mortification in Kendra's face as she looked at him.

"Your parents. She's going to totally embarrass me."

He brought the golf cart to a stop in front of their door, then took her by the shoulders and turned her to face him. "They'll love her because she's your mother."

She shook her head. "Now you're outright lying to me. I've met your parents. They are polite and caring and…and…nice. They'll spend three minutes with her and run the other way."

"Kendra, listen to me. My parents won't break because your mother says things most people don't. My grandmother is like that, and we all do just fine."

Her eyes rounded. "Freak. Tomorrow's the manager's reception. What are we going to do with her while we're hosting our guests? There's no way I'll let her see me nude."

Obviously, his fiancé was going off the deep-end fast and that actually scared him. She'd faced an opinionated sheriff bent on destroying her dream with more backbone than this. "Kendra, listen to me."

She looked at him but she wasn't seeing him.

Screw that. Grasping her by the neck, he pulled her to him and kissed her. It only took a second before she responded. As their tongues entwined, he held her until her hands started to burrow under his shirt.

As much as he wanted to make love to her, they weren't doing it outside on the golf cart and they weren't doing it until he got through to her. Breaking the kiss, he leaned his forehead against hers. "Let's go inside and talk about this calmly, okay?"

She nodded, her breaths already short from her desire.

"Good."

Wedding at Poker Flat
(Poker Flat: Book 5)

Also by Lexi Post

Contemporary Cowboy Romance

Cowboys Never Fold
(Poker Flat Series: Book 1)
Cowboy's Match
(Poker Flat Series: Book 2)
Cowboy's Best Shot
(Poker Flat Series: Book 3)
Cowboy's Break
(Poker Flat Series: Book 4)
Wedding at Poker Flat
(Poker Flat Series: Book 5)
Christmas with Angel
(Last Chance Series: Book 1 & Poker Flat Book 2.5)
Trace's Trouble
(Last Chance Series: Book 2)
Fletcher's Flame
(Last Chance Series: Book 3)
Logan's Luck:
(Last Chance Series: Book 4)
Dillon's Dare
(Last Chance Series: Book 5)
Riley's Rescue
(Last Chance Series: Book 6)
Aloha Cowboy

(Last Chance Series: Book 5.5, Island Cowboy Series: Book 1)

Military Romance

When Love Chimes
(Broken Valor Series: Book 1)
(Prequel to Desires of Christmas Present)
Poisoned Honor
(Broken Valor Series: Book 2) *Coming Soon*

Paranormal Romance

Pleasures of Christmas Past
(A Christmas Carol Series: Book 1)
Desires of Christmas Present
(A Christmas Carol Series: Book 2)
Temptations of Christmas Future
(A Christmas Carol Series: Book 3)
One of A Kind Christmas
(A Christmas Carol Series: Book 4)
On Highland Time
(Time Weavers, Inc. Book 1)
Masque
Passion's Poison
Passion of Sleepy Hollow
Heart of Frankenstein

Sci-fi Romance

Cruise into Eden

Unexpected Eden (The Eden Series: Book 1)
Eden Discovered (The Eden Series: Book 2)
Eden Revealed (The Eden Series: Book 3)
Avenging Eden (The Eden Series: Book 4)
Beast of Eden (The Eden Series: Book 5)
(Eden Series- Tolba: Book 1)

About Lexi Post

Lexi Post is a New York Times and USA Today best-selling author of romance inspired by the classics. She spent years in higher education taking and teaching courses about the classical literature she loved. From Edgar Allan Poe's short story "The Masque of the Red Death" to Tolstoy's War and Peace, she's read, studied, and taught wonderful classics.

But Lexi's first love is romance novels. In an effort to marry her two first loves, she started writing romance inspired by the classics and found she loved it. From hot paranormals to sizzling cowboys to hunks from out of this world, Lexi provides a sensuous experience with a "whole lotta story."

Lexi is living her own happily ever after with her husband and her cat in Florida. She makes her own ice cream every weekend, loves bright colors, and you will never see her without a hat.

Website: www.lexipostbooks.com
Newsletter: http://bit.ly/LexiUpdate
Facebook: https://www.facebook.com/lexipostbooks
Twitter: https://twitter.com/LexiPost
Blog: http://www.happilyeverafterthoughts.com/
Email: lexi@lexipostbooks.com

Made in the USA
Columbia, SC
14 January 2022